The Tea Shop Witch

THE TEA SHOP WITCH
COZY MYSTERY SERIES BOOK ONE

THORA BLUESTONE

Book Description

A disappearing body. Hidden magical talents. An adorable mind-reading dog. And small-town secrets . . .

Addie James's life imploded when she discovered her fiancé cheating and got downsized from her biotech job. So she left Silicon Valley for the haven of her Aunt Kate's tea and apothecary shop in the peaceful mountain town of Stargaze. There, she plans to take a deep breath and figure out what's next.

But when Addie reaches Stargaze, there's no trace of her aunt. Until one night, Aunt Kate's lifeless body shows up and then disappears from the locked shop.

And that's when things *really* start to get strange.

As Addie sets out to find the murderer, she begins to realize her own hidden magical talent is the key to discovering what really happened to her aunt . . . who might not be quite so dead after all.

The problem is, logical Addie isn't sure she can accept the magical parts of herself that science can't explain. Will she learn to embrace this new life that's full of supernatural surprises and solve her aunt's case?

Books by Thora Bluestone

Go to www.ThoraBluestone.com/newsletter to sign up for subscriber-only updates, deals, freebies, and news from Thora!

Contents

Chapter One

ADDIE JAMES WASN'T USUALLY ONE to scream and cry, but she'd spent the past four hundred miles doing both. It was undignified. She was a scientist. A logical person. Not an emotional basket case. But her out-of-character behavior was understandable, seeing as how the previous day had been the worst of her life.

She was in the middle of hoarsely yelling along to the second chorus of "I Will Survive" when there was a low pop under her Ford Escape and the steering wheel pulled to the right.

Her stomach lurched along with the car.

A flat tire. It had to be.

As she slowed and pulled over to the side of the highway, she took a deep breath and let out a long, low moan.

She was less than an hour from Stargaze. So close.

There was a spare in the back, but it was buried under about three hundred pounds of clothes, books, and the few other possessions she'd managed to stuff into her car before fleeing San Francisco.

Reaching for her phone, she tapped pause on the playlist she'd made for this trip, entitled "Jeremy is a Cheating Dirtbag."

She tried to smooth her wind-blown hair, which the rearview mirror revealed to be a tangled mess. Then, heaving a sigh, she killed the engine, got out, and went around to assess the damage.

"Full blowout. Great," she muttered.

At the rear of the car, she opened the hatchback and started pulling out suitcases and bags. She'd barely gotten started with the unpacking when a dented brown pickup with a chugging diesel engine headed the opposite direction swung around and eased to a stop behind her.

She turned and shaded her eyes, wondering if maybe she should have stuck her pepper spray in her pocket. There wasn't much traffic on this two-lane highway.

A head poked out of the pickup's window. It belonged to a guy around her age who wore a hat with the logo of a popular camping-gear company.

"Having car trouble?" he asked.

"Flat tire," she said, trying to determine if his easy smile meant "nice guy" or "crazy kidnapper."

He got out, slammed the door, and walked up to her, his gray-green eyes quickly taking in her wild hair, eyes that were probably red and puffy from crying, and the car that was packed to the gills.

"Let me help," he said, offering another friendly smile. He was cute. Really cute. "It'll go faster with two people."

She almost said no. She knew how to change a flat, and it seemed kind of embarrassing, somehow, to let a complete stranger handle all of her earthly possessions.

"I'm Trey, by the way," he said, offering another smile but not his hand.

Okay, she knew his name, so not a complete stranger. And she liked that he didn't imply she couldn't deal with the situation herself.

"Addie," she said. "And some help would be great, thank you."

Only then did he move closer. Smart guy. He reached for a tote and a duffel bag.

"Coming from somewhere far away?" he asked.

Addie nodded. "California. Bay Area. I've been driving all day. I—I had to get far away as quickly as possible. Not because I did anything bad. I'm not, you know, a criminal on the run or anything." She let out a short laugh. "Well, maybe I'm on the run from my criminally horrible fiancé."

It was a bad joke, but he gave a polite but sympathetic chuckle. "Oh no, what happened?"

"Yesterday I walked in on him with another woman. That was right after I got downsized from my biotech job."

"Wow, I'm sorry to hear that." Trey's eyes softened with sympathy. "What brings you this way?"

"My aunt lives in Stargaze," Addie said. "I'm going to stay with her for a while."

"I just moved to Stargaze," he said, brightening.

"Really? What do you do?"

He leaned into the car to pull out a box. "I'm a musician. A songwriter. Doesn't pay the bills, but maybe someday. Until then, I'm opening a guitar shop. It'll be nice to see a familiar face in Stargaze. Are you planning on staying long?"

She shook her head. "I'm not sure, honestly. Probably not. I'm pretty sure there aren't any biotech jobs in a town that small. I'm just going to chill for a while and figure out what's next."

"Well, it's good to have family to turn to when things get rough."

Addie nearly teared up at how wonderful the kindness of a stranger felt. It didn't hurt that he had nice biceps and soulful eyes.

They finished unpacking the back, and Addie lifted the false trunk bottom to reveal the spare and tire-change kit. She took the jack to the front of the car and set it in place while Trey rolled the tire up.

She let him do most of the rest of the work, suddenly very grateful he was there when she saw how tight the bolts were.

While he finished up with the spare, she wrestled the old tire back into the car and started repacking. Ten minutes later, she was ready to get back on the road.

"I hope to see you around Stargaze," Trey said.

Addie was trying to brush off her hands, but they were too black and filthy from the tire. Having nothing to use to clean them, she wiped her palms down the front of her gray yoga pants.

"Me too," she said, holding out her grimy hand. He gripped it without hesitation, his palm warm and slightly calloused against hers. "Thank you so much for stopping, Trey."

He got back in his truck and waited for her to start her car. Then he pulled onto the highway, headed in the opposite direction she was going.

She turned the music back on, but with the volume way down, and tried calling Aunt Kate. It rang until Addie got voicemail. Weird. She hadn't been able to get a hold of her aunt since the previous day, when Addie had called in tears asking if she could come to Stargaze. Maybe Kate had lost her phone. It wasn't out of the question, as she could be a bit absentminded. Addie left a quick message saying she would arrive within the hour.

As Addie pulled back onto the highway, Taylor Swift began singing about how we were never, ever, ever getting back together.

"That's right, Tay," Addie said. "Jeremy Chasen can go jump out of a plane without a parachute, for all I care. I'm never speaking to him again, no matter how much he begs."

It felt good to make such a declaration, but the truth was, Jeremy probably had no interest in talking to her anyway. He'd barely even gone through the motions of trying to stop Addie from leaving. She'd yanked off her engagement ring and thrown it at him but now wished she would have kept it. It was a very nice ring. She could have pawned it and had enough money for the new mountain bike she'd been eyeing.

Addie had been dating Jeremy for two years and then engaged to him for six months. And now it was all down the drain. Not just her relationship, but also her biotech research job. She'd come home early after getting downsized from the company, and that was when she'd caught Jeremy rolling around with one of their coworkers. Neither of them had lost *their* jobs, which just added insult to injury.

And suddenly, life as Addie knew it was gone. Poof. All in one morning.

She could have stayed in California and found another job, but she needed a break. She needed to be with someone who loved her in a place where she had happy memories. There would be jobs waiting out there when she was ready. Or maybe she could go to medical school like she'd dreamed of when she was younger. At twenty-six, she certainly wasn't too old to do it.

But those were decisions for later. Right now, she just wanted to get to Aunt Kate's shop, Wild Rose Teas and Apothecary, and decompress.

When Addie reached gorgeous little Jade Lake just south of town, her shoulders lowered a few inches as she relaxed a bit. Growing up, she'd spent a month each summer with Aunt Kate. Well, except for the one summer in high school when her parents wouldn't let her go. They'd had a dustup with Kate over some things her aunt had been teaching her. Aunt Kate was into some . . . interesting practices and out-there ideas that Addie's dad, especially, wasn't crazy about. In any case, the times with her aunt had always been nothing but happiness and fun.

As Addie pulled into Stargaze and recognized familiar landmarks, her mood lifted, and a little smile tugged at her lips.

She couldn't wait to reach Kate's shop, sit down with a cup of jasmine green, and pour her heart out to a sympathetic ear.

When Addie found a parking spot right in front of the shop's door, she eagerly looked into the storefront.

It was still a couple of hours before the end of the business day, but the shop was dark. The "Closed" sign hung in the window.

With a frown, Addie shut off the engine.

She got out, peered into the store, and then knocked loudly on the glass.

Something didn't seem quite right. Aunt Kate didn't randomly close Wild Rose in the middle of business hours. And Kate knew Addie would be arriving that afternoon.

Just as Addie pulled out her phone to try her aunt again, a bubbly voice called her name.

"Addie, is that you?"

Addie turned and then grinned as happiness flooded through her on a warm wave.

"Chelsea!" Addie called, going to meet her old friend.

The pretty blond woman let out a happy shriek, did a little skipping hop, and threw her arms around Addie's neck. The smell of an exotic, flowery perfume filled her nose, and the fabric of Chelsea's white bohemian skirt brushed Addie's bare ankles.

"Yesterday Kate told me you were coming," Chelsea said, pulling back. Her dangly metal earrings made cheerful little tinkling noises when she moved. "I thought I saw you drive by, so I ran over here to see. I'm so stoked you're here! It'll be just like old times. We can go camping at the lake, go for hikes, make s'mores. Well, I'm gluten-free now, so I guess I can't have graham crackers. But why am I talking about gluten? Don't listen to me. I'm babbling."

Addie let out a laugh, and something seemed to loosen in her chest. It felt like she hadn't laughed in a year. Chelsea had always been a walking ray of sunshine and one of the best parts of Addie's stays in Stargaze.

"I'm *so* glad to see you," Addie said. "You have no idea."

Chelsea's sun-kissed face sobered. "Kate told me things took a bad turn for you in San Francisco."

Addie snorted. "That's an understatement. I can tell you about it later, but I'd rather not go full buzzkill right off the bat." She glanced into the dark shop again. "Have you seen my aunt? I've been trying to call her all day and she hasn't picked up. It's not like her to close the store during business hours, either."

"Knowing her, she's probably off helping someone," Chelsea said. "You know how she's always got a cause or two."

It was true. Stargaze wasn't a huge city, but it still had its share of people in need. Aunt Kate frequently volunteered at the soup kitchen, and she was on the board of an organization that advocated for women and children.

"Maybe you're right," Addie said. "Maybe there was some sort of emergency."

"Why don't we walk a bit, and I can show you what's changed since you were here last," Chelsea suggested. "We can ask around and see if anyone knows where she is."

"That sounds good," Addie said. "After sitting for eight hours, I need to stretch my legs, anyway. Let me just try her one more time."

Again, Kate's number went to voicemail. Addie left another message saying that she'd arrived.

Then, Chelsea linked her arm through Addie's, aimed south, and began the tour.

On the surface, it might have appeared that artsy, whimsical Chelsea didn't have much in common with logical, intellectual Addie. But their friendship was cemented the summer Addie was twelve years old and went with Kate to Jade Lake for the day. While venturing around the edge of the water looking for frogs, Addie had stumbled upon Chelsea and some other girls. The girls, three of them, had cornered Chelsea in the trees and were taunting her and calling her names.

Addie had picked up a fallen tree branch and charged at them, yelling like a crazy person. She was usually on the quiet side but being in a different place where people wouldn't know that she wasn't normally so bold somehow gave her courage.

It'd been enough to startle the girls, who'd taken off. From that day on, Addie and Chelsea had been "summer best friends," as they used to say when they were kids.

"You know Zelda?" Chelsea said, tipping her head at the large antique store that was immediately to the right of Kate's shop.

"Of course," Addie said.

Zelda's A to Z Antiques had been there even longer than Wild Rose Teas and Apothecary.

Chelsea pushed open the door, and the bells on the handle tinkled. The lower floor of the store was packed with furniture, art, and other large items. In the center was an island formed by four waist-high glass jewelry cabinets arranged in a square.

The sheer volume of merchandise in the store was overwhelming, and Addie nearly groaned at the thought of having to dust all that stuff.

"Zelda," Chelsea called. "Are you in here?"

A head poked up from the middle of the jewelry island. Zelda blinked a few times and adjusted her large-framed glasses on her nose. She had a lot more gray streaking her braid than Addie remembered from her last visit.

For a long moment, Zelda just stared at them. The silence started to feel awkward.

Chelsea stepped forward. "Um, it's me, Chelsea Spring?"

"Oh, yes, Chelsea," Zelda said, giving her head a little shake. She stepped out of the jewelry area and came toward them.

Zelda looked at Addie but barely reacted.

"And you remember Kate's niece, Addie?" Chelsea prompted.

The older woman stopped short. A frown crossed her face.

"Addie, of course. In my mind, you're still a little girl with pigtails," Zelda said, suddenly seeming agitated.

"It's nice to see you, Zelda," Addie said, though the woman's reaction seemed a bit off. It'd only been two years since Addie's last visit, and she'd spent quite a lot of time chatting with Zelda then and in past trips to Stargaze. "Have you seen my aunt today, by chance? The tea shop is closed. Do you know where she might be?"

The previous frown returned and deepened into a scowl, and Zelda's gaze skittered away to a corner of the crowded room. "Haven't seen her or talked to her. I need to get back to work." She turned abruptly and went quickly toward the stairs leading to the upper floor of the store.

Addie cast a confused look at Chelsea, but her friend was squinting after the older woman.

"There's something off in her . . ." Chelsea trailed off softly.

"Oh, c'mon. Just say it," Addie whispered, giving her friend a wry look.

Chelsea gave her a wide-eyed look of innocence. "What?"

"You were going to say her aura, weren't you? There's something off in her aura?"

With a sheepish shrug, Chelsea nodded. "Yeah. But I know you don't like it when I talk about . . . those kinds of things."

Chelsea and Aunt Kate had always had "those kinds of things" in common—they could talk about auras, crystals, dream interpretation, and the like all day long. Addie had listened with interest when she was younger, and even joined in, but since she'd decided as a high school senior to pursue a career in science, such conversations made her want to roll her eyes.

"Well, I don't need to be able to read auras to know that was weird," Addie said. "Zelda barely seemed to know who we were. And she seemed pretty distressed when I brought up Aunt Kate."

"She did," Chelsea agreed, her expression troubled. She forced a smile that wasn't completely convincing. "Let's continue on, shall we?"

They went to the corner to cross the street to the row of stores on the other side of the block. Facing Zelda's antique store was a coffee shop and bakery that Addie didn't remember.

"La Petite Patisserie?" Addie read the sign.

"Ugh, that's Lisette's coffee and pastry shop," Chelsea said with a groan. She hooked Addie's elbow and sped up.

"Lisette?" Addie asked. "Not *that* Lisette."

"Oh, yes. *That* Lisette." Chelsea gave a dramatic roll of her eyes. "That awful girl who went rounds with me for years. She's Lisette Dubois-Kumar now."

Lisette Dubois had been one of the girls Addie had chased off that day by the lake.

"Didn't she move to Portland partway through high school?" Addie asked.

"Best day of my life," Chelsea said. "But she moved back like a year ago with her perfect little family, and she just opened this place. Her BFF is the mayor's wife Yuma, which somehow just makes things even worse."

She was trying to drag Addie faster past the windows of La Petite Patisserie, but Addie wanted a peek inside. The place was decked out in a Parisian farmhouse style, with pretty chandeliers, white painted pedestal tables, a long wooden butcher block table with an old-fashioned cash register, upholstered furniture in little conversation arrangements, and copper cookware hanging on the wall behind the counter. It was undeniably tasteful.

"Wow, all of that must have cost a fortune," Addie remarked.

"Yeah, I think the money she put out to get up and running was a major overreach, though," Chelsea said.

The slim brunette woman placing croissants into the glass case happened to look up and catch sight of them through the window. Addie recognized a more grown-up version of one of Chelsea's tormentors. Lisette still had the same pinch-mouthed expression Addie remembered.

"Oh, shoot," Chelsea muttered. "She saw us."

Lisette stomped to the door and pushed it open, coming out to the sidewalk and facing them, hands on hips. Her cheeks were flushed, her brown eyes flashing, and her angry glare was trained on Addie.

Chapter Two

"I REMEMBER YOU. YOU'RE KATE James's niece," Lisette said, glaring at Addie.

Addie's heart gave an uneasy lurch as she pulled back, caught off guard by Lisette's vehemence.

"Yes, I am," Addie said. "We're looking for my aunt, actually. Have you seen her?"

"I wish," Lisette said. One of her arms flew out in an angry gesture toward Wild Rose Teas and Apothecary across the street. "I've got a bone to pick with her, and she's avoiding me."

"What's the problem?" Addie asked.

Lisette threw up her hands. "Your aunt is ruining my business," she said, as if it should have been obvious.

Sheesh. What was with all the arm waving? So much drama. Addie seriously doubted her aunt would ruin anyone's business. Kate had always been the one to coordinate promotions with her neighbors and find ways to bring more customer traffic to their block, which was beyond the edge of what was considered prime location in downtown Stargaze.

Addie shook her head. "I have no idea what you're talking about, but I'm sure it was just a misunderstanding."

"Oh, come off it, Lisette," Chelsea said. "Kate isn't ruining your business. If you go under, you did it to yourself. Leave Addie alone."

She didn't wait for a response, instead pulling Addie along with her as she quickly walked away.

"Don't mind her," Chelsea said. Her face had gone pale, except for a bright-pink splotch of agitation on each cheek. "It's best to just keep away. She's stressed out over the business, and when Lisette gets upset . . . well, like I said, you just wanna steer clear."

Chelsea seemed genuinely rattled despite her attempt at reassurance.

With a frown, Addie pulled out of Chelsea's grip and stopped. They stood just out of view of La Petite Patisserie's windows, and the irate owner had retreated inside.

Running a hand over her long auburn hair, still a bit frizzed out from the long car ride with the windows down, Addie shook her head. First Zelda seemed agitated at the mention of Aunt Kate, and then Lisette appeared downright angry about something Kate had apparently done to affect Lisette's business. It was so odd. Everyone loved Aunt Kate.

Addie was just about to say as much when a woman in a red floral muumuu, bright-blue eyeshadow, and hair pulled into a tight bun on top of her head leaned out of the door that read "Astrology, Tarot & Palm Reading" in ornate font. A neon sign of a hand with a third-eye symbol on the palm blinked on and off in the window next to the door.

"Betty!" Addie exclaimed joyfully.

The large woman enfolded Addie into a comforting hug that smelled of incense and rose water.

"And Chelsea, I haven't seen you in weeks, dearie," Betty said.

"Oh, I know, it's been too long," Chelsea said. "I need to schedule a reading with you."

Betty held Addie at arm's length and looked her up and down. "What a lovely young woman you've grown up to be." She took Addie's hand in a practiced gesture, turning it palm up and giving it a quick but sharp-eyed scan. "It's been a long time since you let me do a reading for you, dearie. You should come sit at Betty's table. I could do your natal chart."

True to the sign on her door, Betty made her living doing astrology, palm, and tarot readings. When Addie was a child, she loved to sit across from Betty at the table where she saw clients. Chelsea would come, too, and the three of them would have little tea parties if Betty wasn't busy. But as Addie got older, she grew more skeptical of the mysticism and preferred to just chat with Betty instead.

"I'd love to catch up with you," Addie replied, side-stepping the question of doing an astrology reading and gently taking her hand back. "But I haven't been able to get a hold of my aunt today, and I'm starting to get concerned. Do you know where she is?"

Betty gave Addie a reassuring smile. "Probably rescuing cats from trees and the like, you know how she is. I'm sure she'll be back soon. Why don't you girls come in for a moment? I brought lemon bars today. Unless you just came from the Patisserie, in which case you probably don't want anything to eat. Lisette may not smile much, but it's worth staying on her good side for the croissants alone. Mmm-mmm."

"Oh no, we didn't get anything next door. We could come in for just a minute," Addie said.

Chelsea nodded, casting a glance in the direction of La Petite Patisserie and wrapping her arms tightly around her middle. She seemed eager to get off the sidewalk and into Betty's "emporium," as the mystic liked to call her shop.

The lights were low inside. The table where Betty did readings was set up toward the back, hidden by a privacy screen so people on the street couldn't gawk. The front of the store had a miniature living room arrangement on the right, complete with a recliner where Betty often sat as she waited for clients, a thick rug in dark jewel tones, and a table that always had tea and coffee ready. There was even a mini fridge on the floor under the table, hidden behind the tablecloth, where Betty kept cans of sparkling water, bottles of flavored creamer, heavy cream, and an extra supply of whatever treat she'd recently baked at home.

To the left were shelves displaying all manner of occult items, from oracle cards to incense to crystals to candles. There were even a few crystal balls of various sizes, which Betty called "scrying orbs."

The deep thumping bass of rock music rattled the paintings on the wall above the recliner, and Betty cast a frown that way.

Addie didn't want to linger in the emporium—Aunt Kate's absence was really starting to gnaw at her—but felt comforted by familiar surroundings.

"That must be your car across the street," Betty said. "Are you staying a while?"

"I don't know how long, but yeah, it may be an extended stay."

The mystic held up a plump index finger. "Oh! I just remembered, I've got a spare key to Wild Rose," she said. "Let me get it for you, and you can at least move your things into Kate's apartment."

"That would be great," Addie said with relief.

If she could get inside the shop, maybe she could find something that would tell her where her aunt was.

Turning toward the back of the emporium, Betty waved her hand at the tea and coffee service on the table. "Help yourselves to whatever you'd like, dearies. Lemon bars are in the mini fridge."

Chelsea, still seeming distracted, went for one of the lemon bars, but Addie wasn't in the mood to eat or drink anything.

"Hey, I thought you were gluten free," Addie said, peering at the treat in her friend's hand. "Doesn't the crust have flour in it?"

Stopping mid-chew, Chelsea's eyes popped wide. "Oh, crap, I'm such a ditz." She shoved the remaining bar into Addie's hand. "Here, you eat the rest."

Not wanting to waste the lemon bar, Addie reluctantly finished it off.

Betty returned and held out a key ring that had a little enamel teacup charm and one key on it. "You remember the security code in case she has the alarm set?" she asked Addie.

"I do, and thank you so much." Addie looked anxiously out the window at Wild Rose Teas and Apothecary, which was directly across the street from the emporium. "If you don't mind, we'll head over there now. Maybe Aunt Kate left me a note or something."

"Yes, of course, dearie," Betty said. "Come back and see Betty once you're settled."

Chelsea and Addie waved their goodbyes and departed.

Instead of backtracking past La Petite Patisserie, Chelsea pointed ahead. "Let's go that way, and real quick I'll fill you in on what's what for that end of the block."

Next to Betty's emporium was a store called Ripped that occupied a small retail space. It was obviously the source of the loud music that was shaking Betty's wall.

"This place is about a year old," Chelsea said, speaking in a low voice as they passed. "It's owned by that guy in there at the counter, Lance, and it basically caters to gym rats."

Addie gave her a questioning look.

"You know, he sells protein powder in those huge containers, protein bars, and all sorts of supplements that are supposed to get you swole." Chelsea struck a flexed arm pose. "Lance's girlfriend Georgia is usually hanging around too, though I don't see her now. I've tried to talk to her, but she always kind of blows me off. They moved here from Southern California."

Addie jumped a little as the door swung open and a short, muscular guy with a buzz cut came out. Metal music blared from within the store, and Addie caught a glimpse of Lance behind the cash register. He wore a backward baseball hat and a t-shirt with sleeves rolled up, seemingly to show off his muscles.

The guy who'd just left Ripped gave Chelsea and Addie each a once over from head to toe. His eyes lingered on Chelsea's chest.

"Good afternoon, ladies," he said in a tone that he probably thought sounded smooth.

Blech.

Addie guessed he was four or five years younger than her, and he certainly met Chelsea's description of a swole gym rat—bulging calves and arms, not a whole lot of neck, and what looked like a ten-pound barrel of some sort of powder labeled "Muscle Cut Shake Mix" under his arm.

"Hi," Chelsea replied without much enthusiasm and kept going. Once they were in the clear, she said to Addie, "That was Enzo. He's Antonio's nephew who just came here from New York last week."

Addie squinted, reaching back in her memory. "Antonio's the one with the pizza place, right?"

Chelsea nodded. Her voice dropped. "Yeah. Rumor is, Enzo just finished serving time."

"For what?"

"Robbery, I think. I heard he's trying to save enough money for a plane ticket back to New York as soon as possible. His uncle is trying to give him a new start, but small-town life in Oregon isn't Enzo's thing, apparently."

And, obviously, neither was treating women with respect.

They'd reached the corner, and Addie paused with her brows raised. "This space was empty, too, last time I was here." She looked into a hip hair salon with a black and white tile floor.

"You know Javier's, right?" Chelsea asked.

Addie nodded enthusiastically. "It's only my favorite Mexican food in Stargaze."

Mmm . . . Javier's chicken mole tacos. Her mouth watered just thinking about them. Javier Hernandez was the proprietor of his self-named restaurant, which was a family business right around the corner from Aunt Kate's shop.

"This salon is owned by Octavia and Renaldo."

"Oh yeah, the oldest kids in the Hernandez family," Addie said. "I remember them."

A curvy Latina woman five or six years older than Addie was in the salon, called Hair Affair, was applying color to the roots of a client. Octavia smiled and waved the color brush. Chelsea waved back.

"I get my hair done here. Octavia is amazing," Chelsea said. Her grin dimmed a little, and she lowered her voice to a whisper. "But Javier and Sofia, the parents, weren't too thrilled about losing two of their kids to a new business. Still some tension there."

"Oh, that's too bad," Addie said, but she couldn't help looking distractedly at Wild Rose Teas and Apothecary.

She didn't want to be rude, but she was eager to use the key Betty had given her.

Chelsea noticed her impatience. "We can finish the tour some other time," she said. She pointed at the large building kitty-corner to Hair Affair. "That's Grinning Catfish, a new microbrewery and restaurant started by two guys from Seattle. We'll have to grab a bite there sometime."

"Sure," Addie said, picking up her pace as they crossed the street.

They passed a bookstore called Enchanted Pages and then a small retail space that looked like it was under construction.

By the time they reached Wild Rose, Addie's pulse was tapping with anticipation. She unlocked the door, and since there was no warning series of beeps, she knew the alarm wasn't armed.

"Aunt Kate?" she called out in a hopeful tone.

No answer.

"I'm going to check upstairs," Addie said.

Flipping on lights, she headed through the store, absently noting that her aunt had added a small seating area with four little café tables near the widest window. She stopped at the counter briefly to see if there was a note, but there was nothing next to the register except the dog-eared spiral notebook her aunt kept, where she made notes about apothecary remedies for clients. Addie had peeked in it when she was younger, but Aunt Kate had wisely coded her entries so clients couldn't be identified. Addie continued past shelves lined with jars containing all kinds of loose teas and herbs, amber dropper bottles of tinctures, and other apothecary items.

Stairs at the back led up to the apartment where her aunt lived. It only took a minute to scan the kitchenette, living area, bedroom, and bathroom to see no one was there.

Disappointed, but not really surprised to find no sign of her aunt, Addie returned downstairs. She and Chelsea went out to Addie's Ford Escape and began unpacking. Addie had mostly brought only clothes, books, her laptop, toiletries, and a few boxes of hastily packed things that had some personal meaning to her. Furniture, kitchen items, and anything else that wouldn't fit in her car she'd left behind at the apartment she'd shared with Jeremy. It would cost a lot to replace it when she eventually got her own place, but at the time she'd left, she was too distraught to try to divide all that stuff. Besides, who wanted reminders of their dirtbag, cheating ex around?

Forty-five minutes later, after Addie's possessions had been neatly arranged in the living room upstairs, she and Chelsea ordered a gluten-free pizza from Slice of Pie.

Enzo, the guy they'd run into outside Ripped, delivered it.

"Delicious authentic New York pie for two beautiful ladies," he said with a wide grin.

His gaze turned shrewd and flitted past Addie, taking in the store in a way that made her uneasy.

She pushed some cash at him and grabbed the box out of his hand. "Thanks for the delivery," she said in a tone that she hoped made it clear she wasn't in the mood to chat.

He seemed to get the message and backed away. Addie closed the door and locked it, and she and Chelsea dug into the delicious pizza.

Afterward, they chatted for a while, catching each other up on recent events in their lives. Chelsea had opened a boutique clothing store not far away, just inside the prime location area of downtown.

"Lisette was looking for retail space at the same time," she said. "She wanted the space I ended up with but couldn't quite afford it. Yet another reason she hates me."

"I'd love to see your store," Addie said and then yawned so wide her jaw cracked.

Chelsea patted her hand. "I'll show you soon, hon." She stood up and stretched. "You're exhausted, so I'm gonna stop my jabbering and let you relax. I know you're worried about your aunt, but I'm sure she's all right. I bet she'll show up tonight."

Addie walked Chelsea to the front of the store and let her out. Back upstairs, she surveyed her things and then started digging around for sweats. She changed and then settled on the daybed that had always been the place she slept when she visited, and which doubled as living room seating, and tried calling Aunt Kate one more time.

No answer.

Maybe Chelsea was right, and Kate would show up later.

Addie got comfortable and idly flipped through apps on her phone. Her eyelids grew heavy, and she closed them, only intending to rest for a few minutes.

Some time later, she woke with a start, her heart lurching and then pounding against her ribs.

There'd been a noise.

Addie rose and stood rigidly still, listening.

There was a grunt, some shuffling, a loud thump, and then the sound of a heavy object hitting the floor.

Cold sweat prickled down Addie's back as she crept to the top of the stairs.

Chapter Three

"AUNT KATE?" ADDIE WHISPERED TOWARD the stairs.

She didn't want to holler because she had a funny feeling it wasn't her aunt making all that noise down there. With her phone gripped tightly in her damp hand, she started creeping down, one slow step at a time.

There were more scuffling noises. A clanging crash.

She should have grabbed the pepper spray out of her purse but didn't want to take the time to go back.

Halfway down, Addie plucked up her courage.

"Who's down there?" she demanded in as commanding a voice as she could muster. "Identify yourself, or I'm calling 911. Also, I've got a gun."

She rolled her eyes at herself. *Also, I've got a gun?* Real convincing.

But it must have worked because there were quick retreating footsteps. Then silence.

Addie hurried down to the bottom of the stairs and flipped on the shop lights.

Blinking in the sudden brightness, it took her a second to absorb the scene.

She gasped, her phone slipping from her hand and hitting the floor.

There was a motionless body on the floor next to the register counter. And whoever it was had hair the exact sun-streaked light-brown shade as Aunt Kate.

"Oh no," Addie breathed and then rushed forward.

Going around so she could see the woman's face, Addie fell to the floor. It was Kate.

Addie shook her aunt's shoulder. "Aunt Kate."

No response. But there was blood smeared on the floor under her aunt's temple. With trembling fingers, Addie tried to find a pulse on the side of Kate's neck. Addie couldn't feel one, but maybe it was because she was shaking so badly.

Addie scrambled for her phone, dialed 911, and raced out the front of the store, hoping there might be someone who could help her.

As she frantically looked up and down the dark street, she told the operator to send an ambulance to Wild Rose Teas and Apothecary.

The operator was trying to ask Addie questions, but she was barely paying attention. She lowered the phone.

"Help!" she shouted frantically down the street. "Please, I need help!"

But the storefronts were all dark, and no one was around.

She wheeled around and raced back to the door. Dread curled in her gut as she tried to steel herself to start CPR on her aunt. A long-buried memory of another unconscious person rose up, and she froze with her hand on the door's handle.

No, she couldn't let the past prevent her from helping her aunt.

Addie pushed inside.

A few steps into the shop, she stopped short with a gasp.

No one was there.

Addie ran forward and then spun around in a full circle. "Aunt Kate?"

She turned toward the front of the store. Could her aunt have snuck past her? Impossible.

Someone appeared at the door, and Addie let out a little shriek of surprise.

The door swung open, and a young man dressed in nothing but cutoff sweats stood there.

Addie just stared at him, for a split second immobilized by confusion as she stared at the guy who'd helped her with the flat tire. "Trey?"

His eyes widened in surprise.

"Addie?" he said.

"What are you doing here?" she asked in confusion.

"I'm leasing the space next door and I live upstairs. Was that you calling for help?"

"My aunt was here," Addie said. She was breathing hard, as if she'd just jogged around the block. She pointed to the floor, and her hand trembled. "She was lying there unconscious. I couldn't find a pulse. There was blood under her head."

Trey strode forward in bare feet and came to examine the spot Addie indicated. He crouched down.

"I feel like I'm going crazy," Addie said, clutching her phone tightly with one hand and pushing the fingers of her other hand into her hair. "She was there, and there was blood, and I think—I think she was *dead*."

Trey looked up at her. "The blood's still there." He rose and touched her shoulder. "Try to take slow breaths."

She nodded and looked again at the floor. He was right about the blood. But what'd happened to Aunt Kate? Addie's gaze traveled to the rear of the store.

"Could you stay here and watch for the ambulance?" she asked. "I'm going to check the back door."

"Of course," he said.

She hurried past the storage room to the door that led out to the alley and pushed it open. During business hours, it was left unlocked on the inside as a fire exit but always locked from the outside so no one could sneak in through the back.

As the wail of a siren grew louder, Addie swung her gaze up and down the alley. Aunt Kate's Subaru was parked there in its usual spot next to a dumpster.

"Aunt Kate!" Addie yelled. "Are you out here?"

She ran around the car and then checked on the other side of the dumpster, just in case Kate had stumbled outside and then collapsed. But no one was there.

Except for more trash bins, the alley was empty.

The door had closed and locked behind Addie, and she was just about to race down the alley and around to the front when Trey appeared, holding the door open.

"The ambulance is here," he said. "I called the police, too."

Dazed, she followed him back inside.

Two paramedics were standing in the shop, holding some equipment and looking around with confused expressions. The rotating red and white lights on top of the ambulance swept across the front windows.

Addie shook her head. "She was here. She was right here."

"I checked the rest of the store," Trey said. "I didn't see any sign of anyone."

"No more blood?"

He shook his head. "I'm going to ask the paramedics to wait outside, just in case."

"Okay, thank you."

Just as the paramedics retreated to their ambulance, a police car pulled up outside.

Addie went to the door, which had been propped open, to meet the officer. His nametag said Officer Davis, and he reminded her of a young Morgan Freeman.

"Evening," he greeted her, his brows knit in concern. "What seems to be the trouble?"

She recounted how she'd been awakened by noises and came downstairs to find her unresponsive aunt. Leading the officer to the spot near the register, she pointed out the small pool of blood on the floor.

"But she's gone," Addie said. "I checked the alley. There's no sign of her."

Officer Davis puffed his cheeks and blew out a breath. "Are you positive you weren't dreaming?"

She pulled back, a little offended by his suggestion. "Absolutely positive. There's *blood*." She pointed again.

He nodded and began carefully walking around, bent over at the waist as he examined the floor. When he looked behind the counter, he straightened.

"Was the register like this before?" he asked.

Addie went to stand next to him. The cash register had been knocked onto the floor. It sat on its side with the drawer open, and it appeared to be empty.

"No, it was definitely on the counter earlier," she said.

He peered at the counter. "There's a bit of hair and blood on the corner."

"That must be where Aunt Kate hit her head," Addie said weakly.

She shivered as a scenario began to form in her mind. Maybe Kate had come home late and someone had followed her inside to rob the shop. There'd been a scuffle, and her aunt had banged her head hard on the counter, knocking her out. The robber took the money from the register and ran.

It was a rational explanation, except . . . where was Aunt Kate?

Addie's throat went dry. "Do you think—do you think when I was outside, the robber came back and took her . . ." She trailed off in a whisper.

"You said you heard the suspected assailant leave, didn't you?" Officer Davis asked.

She nodded.

"And the back door is locked from the outside?"

"Yes," she said. "It's always locked from the outside."

"Then the assailant couldn't have come back in that way. Though I suppose he or she could have propped it open. There's no other way into this shop?"

"Just the front door and the alley door," she confirmed.

"Was the front door locked?"

Addie's stomach clenched. She thought she'd checked the deadbolt before she went upstairs for the night, but then when she'd run out to find help, she'd just pushed it open. It hadn't been deadbolted.

She scrunched her face. "I—I don't think so."

"Okay, well, I'm going to get on the horn to the station and have a detective come out," he said. He walked away, talking into his cell phone.

Trey, who'd been standing nearby, came up to Addie.

"Is there someone I can call for you?" he asked, his gray-green eyes concerned. "Another family member?"

Addie let out a breath. "I'll call Chelsea. Thank you so much for coming over. You don't have to stay, if you don't want to."

"I don't mind," he said. His eyes were gorgeous, with those long, dark lashes, some part of Addie's awareness noticed. "I'll just run next door for some clothes and shoes, and I'll be right back."

She managed a faint smile. "Okay, thanks."

Chelsea answered on the fourth ring, and Addie quickly explained what was going on.

"I'll be there in ten minutes," her friend promised. Earlier that evening, Chelsea had mentioned she'd bought a cottage north of downtown, not far from Wild Rose. "No, screw the speed limit. Make that five minutes."

When she arrived at the shop, dressed in a pink designer sweat-suit and white sneakers, makeup-less and with her blond hair sleep-messed, she ran to Addie and claimed her in a tight hug.

"It's going to be okay," Chelsea whispered soothingly.

Addie took a deep breath to ward off the tears that threatened, and she nodded against Chelsea's shoulder.

Officer Davis asked them to move outside so they wouldn't interfere with the crime scene.

Trey showed up, in jeans, a zip-up hoodie thrown over a t-shirt, and flipflops.

Addie quickly introduced him to Chelsea, who gave him a quick and approving look.

"I knew someone got that space recently, but I wasn't sure who. What kind of business are you planning to open?" she asked, glancing at the storefront next to Wild Rose.

"It'll be a guitar shop," he said. "Possibly with a small stage at the back for live acoustic performances. I've barely started on the interior, though."

His voice was deep and resonant, with just the barest hint of rasp. Maybe he was a singer as well as a musician and songwriter.

He turned to Addie. "I met your aunt for the first time last week, and she seems like a wonderful person."

She gave him a grateful smile, not just for the kind comment, but also for not using past tense when he spoke of Aunt Kate.

"She is," Addie said. "She's the best."

Before she could get emotional, a sedan pulled up behind Officer Davis's car, and a woman in dark jeans, a light coat, and a baseball cap mashed over her curly red-orange hair got out. She spoke briefly to the officer, who pointed at Addie.

The woman walked purposefully over. "Addison James?"

Addie nodded.

"I'm Detective Julia McCann." The woman showed a gleaming badge. "Would you mind telling me what happened here tonight?"

"Sure," Addie said. "I was upstairs asleep on the daybed—"

Detective McCann cut her off. "Let's go sit in my car, if you don't mind."

"Okay," Addie said reluctantly, not happy about leaving the comfort of Chelsea's protective arm around her shoulders.

Addie shivered and followed the detective. Something warm draped across her back, and she turned to see that Trey had caught up with her and given her his hoodie.

"Thank you," she said gratefully.

She went around to the passenger side of Detective McCann's car and got in. It had that chemical new-car smell that always gave Addie a headache. The interior wasn't just spotless, but also completely devoid of anything personal except for a school picture of a grinning red-haired boy around nine or ten years old taped to the dash.

"Okay," the detective said, opening a little notebook. "Start at the beginning. Don't leave out any details, even things you think are insignificant."

Again, Addie recounted the entire story.

Detective McCann listened and made notes, remaining unexpressive the entire time.

"Was your aunt having any trouble lately? Disagreements? Money issues? Arguments with a significant other?"

Addie wasn't sure what that might have to do with anything. The cash register had been emptied. The incident seemed like a robbery. Or maybe someone had only wanted it to look that way?

Addie opened her mouth, ready to say that her aunt had no enemies or money issues but hesitated when she recalled her earlier encounters with Zelda and Lisette.

"My aunt isn't in a relationship that I'm aware of," Addie said. "And she's always been really responsible with money."

The detective's eyes sharpened. "Disagreements?"

"I don't think—well, actually, earlier today the woman who owns that French bakery and coffee shop seemed agitated about something related to my aunt," Addie said slowly. "But everyone has always loved her. She's always gotten along with everybody. She has a big heart, and she loves to help people. She feeds the homeless, for goodness sake."

"Yes, I'm aware of your aunt's community involvement," Detective McCann said and then pursed her lips into a hard line.

Addie frowned. The detective said "community involvement" as if it were a thing to be suspicious of. And Addie got the feeling this woman knew her aunt better than she was letting on and wasn't Kate's biggest fan.

"What exactly did the woman at the French bakery say?" the detective pressed.

"That my aunt was ruining her business," Addie said reluctantly. "But Kate would never do a thing like that. It has to be some sort of misunderstanding."

Detective McCann wrote several words in her little notebook. "Did she happen to leave behind her purse, phone, or anything else of that nature?" she asked.

"No, I don't think so," Addie said. "Like I said, I'd been trying to call her all day. Maybe she lost her phone or the battery went dead."

"Okay." The detective flipped her notebook closed with a crisp movement. "My colleague should be here any minute. We're going to take pictures and collect evidence from the crime scene. Stay close in case we have questions."

"Wait," Addie said. "Do you have any idea what might have happened to her? Any theories?"

"We need more information," Detective McCann said in a clipped tone and then got out of the car.

Addie slowly followed, going back to huddle with Chelsea and Trey.

"How did it go?" Chelsea asked.

For a moment, Addie chewed her lower lip as her gaze tracked Detective McCann inside the shop.

"It was . . . odd," Addie said. "I'm getting the impression there are things about Aunt Kate I didn't know. And maybe those things caught up with her tonight."

But secrets or no, where the heck had Kate disappeared to after she'd collapsed on the floor?

Chapter Four

AFTER THE SCENE HAD BEEN thoroughly documented, Detective McCann warned Addie, Chelsea, and Trey not to speak about the investigation, and then all of the officials finally left.

"Unless there's something else I can do, I'm going to head back to my place," Trey said. "But let me give you my number. Call or knock if you need anything, okay?"

Addie gave him her phone, and he punched in his digits.

"Thank you so much for helping me," she said gratefully. "Again."

He gave her a tired, but warm smile. It wasn't until he was gone that she realized she was still wearing his hoodie.

"Again?" Chelsea echoed. "You met him before?"

"He actually helped me with a flat tire about thirty miles out of town," Addie said.

"Mm, I like him," Chelsea said, glancing at the door.

"Yeah, he's nice," Addie said. Then she shook her head miserably. "I feel like I should do something. Go and look for her, maybe."

"The police already walked around the vicinity to make sure she hadn't collapsed nearby. It's the middle of the night, and you're about to keel over from exhaustion, honey." Chelsea came and held

Addie by the shoulders. "Do you want to spend the rest of the night at my house? This might not be the best place for you right now."

Addie shook her head. "I need to stay. If my aunt comes back, I want to be here."

"Okay, then I'll stay, too," Chelsea said, though Addie could tell by Chelsea's skirting glance around the shop that she seemed a little uneasy about the prospect of staying the night. Her eyes lingered on the crime scene. "Why don't you go upstairs and let me clean up down here?"

Addie's eyes misted at the offer. "That's so sweet of you, but I couldn't let you do that alone."

Together, they scrubbed the floor and corner of the counter with soapy water. Addie picked up the cash register, which was still speckled with powder from being dusted for fingerprints, and set it back on the checkout counter.

After verifying one more time that both doors were locked, Addie led her friend upstairs. They plopped on the daybed, and Addie turned on Netflix. But she couldn't focus on the screen. She just kept replaying what'd happened.

"I froze earlier," Addie said softly after a minute or two.

"What do you mean?" Chelsea asked, turning so she could face Addie.

"I should have started CPR on her as soon as I realized there was no pulse. But I didn't. I panicked."

"That's totally understandable. You didn't do anything wrong."

Addie rubbed her forehead. "No, I froze because, well . . ." She squeezed her eyes closed for a moment.

She really didn't want to tell the story, but she needed to get it out.

"When I was a kid, I wanted to be a doctor," Addie said.

"Yeah, I remember," Chelsea said.

"I took CPR and first responder classes as soon as I was old enough. Then, at the end of ninth grade, I was at a pool party. It was at the house of a girl, Yolanda, I'd known since grade school. I'd gone to her slumber parties for years. Anyway, her dad was making burgers at the barbeque, and he fell. Collapsed. I saw it happen. I ran over there, and I did everything you're supposed to do—rolled him over to his back, checked for breathing and pulse. When he didn't respond, I started CPR. I was the only one there who knew how to do it. The ambulance seemed to take forever to get there." Addie sighed heavily, and her gaze unfocused. "They don't tell you how hard it is to keep up CPR, especially when you're a scrawny kid working on a full-grown man. Toward the end, I just about passed out."

Addie stopped talking, pulled her lips in between her teeth, and bit down hard.

"What happened?" Chelsea asked softly.

"He died. Heart attack," Addie whispered. "It really shook me up. I had nightmares for years about trying to save people. I'd always wanted to become a doctor, but after that . . ." She shook her head slowly. "I couldn't stand the thought of failing to save a life. So, I went into research instead. There are only a couple of people in the world who know the truth about why I chose biotech instead of medicine."

"You did all you could," Chelsea said. "It's not your fault he died."

"But that made me freeze up tonight. For all I know, it cost Aunt Kate her life."

"No," Chelsea said firmly. "I don't believe she's dead."

Addie frowned. "Based on what?"

"A feeling I had when I got here. Rooms can have auras, or energy, just like people. It didn't feel like a room where someone died.

It felt like, well, I don't know exactly—strange. Something intense happened. But not that."

Maybe it was because Aunt Kate had been taken somewhere else and died there. Addie couldn't bring herself to voice the thought. But if that wasn't what happened, where had Kate gone? And why?

Chelsea grasped Addie's arm and pulled her closer, gently urging her to lie down with her head on Chelsea's lap.

"Thank you for being here," Addie said, allowing herself to take comfort in her friend.

"Of course, honey."

After about twenty minutes, Addie looked up. Chelsea's eyes were closed, and she was breathing deeply with her head propped on the fluffy pillow beside her.

It was after two in the morning, but Addie couldn't sleep. Thinking a cup of tea might help, she got up and tiptoed downstairs with her phone in the pocket of Trey's sweatshirt.

With water heating in the electric kettle on the counter under the apothecary shelves, Addie found the jar containing a custom herbal tea her aunt had created called "Restful Blend."

Not bothering to find a tea ball, Addie dropped three generous pinches of the herbs straight into a pretty pale-blue cup with a matching saucer that had a ring of little dolphins around the edge. She set a silver spoon alongside the cup.

While she was waiting for the water to heat, she noticed Aunt Kate had made some changes in the shop. There were two small glass display cases on the counter with crumbs in them. Evidence of baked goodies? The shop had never offered food before, but with the addition of the little seating area, the pastry cases, and stacks of tea cups and saucers, it appeared Kate had expanded the business to make it not just a store, but a tiny café.

Was the change, seemingly an attempt to attract new customers, possibly evidence of money troubles? Or could the investment required for the upgrades have put Aunt Kate in a tight spot?

Addie shook her head. Kate had always been very responsible with her finances. She'd remained in a small retail space even after her business was well established, and she'd preferred to stay in the tiny apartment upstairs because it was so cheap to do so.

No, if her aunt had secrets, they weren't of the money or debt variety. Besides, the overturned cash register and empty drawer pointed to a robbery, not some loan shark coming after Kate.

The button on the electric kettle popped, and Addie poured hot water over the tea leaves. She chose one of the tables and sat down, thinking about her aunt as she waited for the tea to steep. The comforting aromas of chamomile, lavender, peppermint, lemon balm, and other herbs wafted up on the steam.

More than anything, she wished Aunt Kate was sitting across the table. Addie couldn't help replaying the scene from earlier, when she'd come down and discovered her aunt unconscious on the floor.

Who had hurt her? Why had they done it? And where was Aunt Kate now?

The questions swirled in Addie's mind as she looked down into her teacup. She sipped and contemplated, trying to come up with theories about how Kate had disappeared.

When Addie got toward the bottom of the cup, she used the spoon to hold back the loose leaves so she wouldn't swallow them. Still deep in thought, she swirled the leaves in the last bit of liquid.

Then, remembering a little tea-leaf-reading ritual Betty had shown her how to do many years ago, on a whim Addie overturned the cup onto the saucer. She turned the cup right side up and peered into the it.

She gasped as an uncomfortable tingling sensation started in the center of her chest and burst outward through her limbs. The patterns and shapes formed by the soggy tea leaves blurred.

Addie gripped the edge of the table, afraid she might pass out as her heart thumped in alarm. Blinking hard, she tried to clear her vision.

What was happening?

After a few seconds, her eyes focused, but the tingling only got worse. It was almost unbearable, like a swarm of bees buzzing through her veins.

Looking down into the cup, she began to make out shapes. But they weren't just blobs of used tea leaves. They were *objects*, clear as if someone had outlined the details for her in fine-tip marker. And the degree of detail was astonishing, the shapes impossibly intricate yet also unbelievably clear for being so tiny.

Addie shook her head hard. This wasn't possible. She had to be imagining things. Maybe there was something in the tea that caused hallucinations. Or she was having an allergic reaction. Maybe she was still upstairs, dreaming.

Her pulse pounded. She wanted to look away, but somehow couldn't tear her gaze from the little pictures in the tea leaves.

A flower inside a bottle.

A smiling face—no, an entire head—with the shape of a brain floating above it.

A capital L underlined by a slim knife.

Two stick figures with a lightning bolt separating them.

And there was a noise, a quiet sound tickling her eardrums. Addie's breath came faster. The sound was a soft whispering voice.

This wasn't a dream. It was much too vivid. She was definitely awake.

A chill spilled over her scalp and down her spine.

"No," she ground out, shoving the cup away and squeezing her eyes closed.

She pressed her palms against the surface of the table and gulped air, trying to calm her racing heart.

When she finally opened her eyes, the tingling had subsided. The whispers had faded away. And when she dared peek into the cup, all she saw was a mess of soggy herbs and leaves.

Not entirely certain why she was doing it, she reached for her phone and snapped a picture of the cup. Then she took it to the utility sink at the back of the shop and rinsed it out, relieved to see the tea swirling down the drain.

She washed the cup, spoon, and saucer and left them on the drying rack next to the sink.

Suddenly spent, she trudged upstairs, where she found Chelsea still sound asleep. Curling up on the opposite end of the daybed, Addie quickly fell into a blessedly dreamless slumber.

LIGHT PENETRATED ADDIE'S EYELIDS, AND she woke with a start, groaning when she realized how stiff her neck was. Chelsea was curled up on the other end of the daybed, snoring softly. She'd pulled a quilt over her in the night. Addie must have done the same, as she was snuggled under an afghan. She checked her phone. It was seven thirty-five.

The previous day came flooding back, cutting through the fog of sleep. The strange, detailed images in the teacup whirled around in Addie's brain. She flipped to the photos on her phone, thinking maybe she'd dreamed the whole incident.

Nope. There was the picture with the globs of used tea stuck around the inside of the cup. The mental images she'd seen, with the intricate details superimposed on the shapes, appeared in her mind's eye.

She set down her phone and pushed her fingertips into her closed eyelids.

Everything had become so weird. Too weird. Her logical, science-loving brain was not enjoying it one bit.

She pushed the blanket aside and stood.

She didn't want to do it, but she was going to have to make a phone call. Her father, who was Aunt Kate's brother, needed to know that she was missing. He was on a round-the-world cruise with his new wife, whom Addie had only met once before they'd gotten married. Addie hated to be the bearer of bad news, but it needed to be done. She was spared having to tell her mother because she was on an extended yoga retreat in India and wasn't reachable unless Addie called the retreat center. Mom liked Aunt Kate, but after the divorce a couple of years ago, they were no longer family. Addie was going to skip that call for the time being. She didn't want to disturb her mother's retreat.

With a deep breath, Addie went downstairs and found her father's number in her contacts. She wasn't even sure what time zone he was in.

"Hi, pumpkin," he answered on the second ring, clearly surprised she was calling.

"Hi, Dad," Addie said. "I'm sorry to be interrupting your trip, but I thought you'd want to know that Aunt Kate is missing."

"What? Missing?" His surprise turned to confusion.

She sat down at the table where she'd had tea the night before.

"Yeah," Addie said. "I think—well, I think she might be hurt."

She couldn't bring herself to say that she'd seen Aunt Kate's lifeless body and then come back to find it gone.

"Wait, are you in Stargaze?" he asked.

"Oh, right, about that." She pinched the bridge of her nose and as briefly as humanly possible told him why she wasn't in California anymore.

After some awkwardly sympathetic words—Dad had a PhD in statistical modeling and had never been great when it came to things like emotions and failures—he sighed loudly.

"You know your aunt has a way of getting too involved with the bleeding hearts," he said. "Sometimes she doesn't have a whole lot of sense. I'm sure she'll turn up."

Addie frowned. Her father and aunt had always butted heads, but that seemed a little harsh.

"Well, I'll let you know if there are any updates, okay?" Addie said, eager to end the conversation.

"Okay, pumpkin. Enjoy your break. Let me know when you head back to California."

"Um, yeah, will do. Love you."

"Love you."

For some reason, it annoyed Addie that her father assumed she'd be skulking back to her old life. She hadn't ruled out returning to the Bay Area, but she couldn't think about that yet. Especially not with her aunt missing.

Chelsea appeared at the bottom of the stairs. "Hey, how are you doing, hon?"

Addie ran her hand over her hair. "As well as can be expected, I guess. Thank you again for staying last night."

"Of course." She tilted her head and gave Addie a sympathetic look. "What do you want to do now?"

"See if the police have come up with anything. And I'd like to speak to the neighbors in case anyone saw or heard something. I know the detective said we couldn't talk about the case, but there's no way I'm going to just sit by and do nothing."

"I'll help you," Chelsea said firmly. "First, I'm gonna run home and change. Then, I've got to open the boutique. I can leave as soon as Lang shows up. But after that I'm all yours."

Addie gave her a grateful, wobbly smile as she tried not to tear up. "You're amazing."

"Don't worry." Chelsea patted her arm. "Somebody's gotta know something. We just need to figure out who."

Chapter Five

AFTER CHELSEA LEFT, ADDIE MADE a pot of strong coffee and looked up the number for the local police department. She asked for Julia McCann and got transferred, but the detective didn't pick up, so Addie left a message.

Feeling like she hadn't bathed in a week, she was just about to go upstairs for a quick shower when there was a noise at the front door, startling her and sending her pulse skittering. She peered through the glass but didn't see anyone there. She went to the bottom of the stairs.

More scratching.

Addie looked at the door again, this time tilting her gaze down to find a small reddish-brown dog with his paws up on the window and his breath fogging the glass.

She set her coffee down and padded to the front of the shop.

The dog wagged and gave a little yip.

A glance left and right revealed no one nearby, so Addie unlocked the door and opened it. The dog trotted right in, still wagging. He—he? Yes, the dog was definitely a he—came around to Addie, sat, and looked up at her, seeming to give her a big doggie smile.

She closed the door and then knelt down in front of him. He had a collar, and while his hair was just beginning to look a bit shaggy, he looked reasonably cared for and fed.

"Who do you belong to, little guy?"

His tail thumped twice.

Reaching out, she let him sniff her hand and give it a lick before she tried to find a tag on the collar. Locating it, she squinted to read the engraved word.

"Lucky?"

He wagged again.

She turned the tag over. No number or address.

"Are you lost?" she asked.

Lucky tilted his head and peered at her with his brown eyes. He appeared to be a poodle mix of some sort.

She scratched his head and sighed.

"I guess you can hang out with me for now," she said. His ears perked when she spoke. "When I start canvassing the neighborhood, I'll ask around about your owner. But first, I've got to get cleaned up."

When she stood, Lucky did too. He watched her expectantly. She turned and went to find a bowl to fill with water, and he sauntered along at her left heel. Then he followed her upstairs. She set the bowl down, and Lucky sniffed at it and then went to the round rug in front of Aunt Kate's rocking chair, circled twice, and lay down.

"Well, you seem pretty well behaved," Addie said. "Don't prove me wrong while I'm in the shower, okay?"

Lucky wagged and then laid his head down on his paws.

What a cute little guy. Someone had to be missing him.

When Addie emerged from the bathroom wrapped in a towel, Lucky's eyes followed her as she moved across the living room. She stared at the suitcases and bags stacked against the wall.

"Jeans," she muttered. "Where are you, jeans?"

She'd packed in such a rush she had no idea what she'd stuffed where.

The dog went to the largest suitcase and bumped it with his nose. He looked up at her and then repeated the action.

Giving him an amused smile, she placed her hands on her hips. "You think my jeans are in there, huh?"

She unzipped the suitcase and flipped up the top. Her brows rose. Sure enough, right on top was her favorite pair of jeans.

"Find my Nikes, and I'll give you some of the leftover pizza," she said jokingly.

Lucky went around her to the duffel that had often doubled as her gym bag. He pawed at it. When she opened it and peered inside, there were her navy running shoes. Had to be a coincidence, but it was cute and amusing, nonetheless.

She turned to the dog, narrowing her eyes. "Do you understand English?"

He wagged.

"Can you read my mind?"

More wagging.

Addie snorted. "Prove it."

She concentrated, picturing her toothbrush in her mind. She'd been too tired the previous night to find it, and her teeth felt like they were growing fuzz.

Lucky nosed the duffel aside and stuck his head into a tote bag. He came out with the loop of her toiletry kit in his teeth.

Addie's lips parted in surprise as she watched him bring the small bag over and drop it at her feet. Lucky sat and tipped his head back to look at her.

She blinked several times. "That . . . must have been another coincidence." After they stared at each other for an awkward moment, she reached down and patted his soft head. "Seriously, Lucky, don't get spooky on me, okay? I don't need more of that in my life right now."

Trying not to think too hard about what the dog had just done, she got dressed, put on tinted SPF 20 moisturizer and some mascara, brushed her teeth, and pulled her damp auburn hair back into a ponytail.

Pushing her phone into the back pocket of her jeans, she found the key to the shop. Her phone vibrated, and she pulled it out. It was Chelsea.

"Hi," Addie answered. "I was just about to see if you were ready to go."

"I'm so sorry, but I'm going to be another hour or so." Chelsea spoke quickly, sounding frazzled. "My store manager Lang had some car trouble and she's late. I've already got a few customers, so I can't close the boutique."

"No worries. Take care of your business, and catch up with me later if you can. But please, don't stress about it. You've done so much for me already."

"Okay," Chelsea said. "Call me if you hear anything."

"Will do."

Downstairs, Addie got a little corner of the promised pizza from the fridge and fed it to Lucky. But when she tried to leave him inside the shop, he started barking furiously.

She opened the door, and he darted out. Fearing he might run out into the street, her heart jumped. But he didn't. He just raced around her in excited circles. She tried to herd him back inside, but he evaded her attempts.

Finally, she faced off with him, her hands planted on her hips.

"You're not going to let me leave you in there, are you?"

He yipped and hopped.

"Okay, but you have to promise to stay next to me. No running out into the street. If you got hit, I'd never forgive myself."

Lucky quieted, sat, and peered up at her.

"Are you trying to reason with a dog?" asked a rich voice.

Addie looked up to find Trey leaning out the door next to Wild Rose Teas and Apothecary.

She shrugged sheepishly. "Yeah. He showed up this morning, and he won't let me leave him behind. There's no number or address on his tag. Does he look familiar to you?"

Trey shook his head, quirking an amused smile at the little dog. "I've never seen him before. Looks like he wants to be yours now." He sobered, and his gaze met hers. "How are you doing?"

Addie gave a small nod. "Okay. I'm going to walk around the block and see if anyone saw or heard anything. Thank you again for helping me last night. I was kind of a mess."

His face warmed, his gray-green eyes softening. "Don't mention it, I'm glad I was here. Let me know if I can do anything. I'll be here working on the floors all day."

"Thanks," Addie said. When he started to go back inside, she held up her hand and went forward a few steps. "Hey, you haven't seen anything odd around here lately, have you? Or heard anything? Maybe someone arguing with my aunt?"

He shook his head. "I usually have music blasting while I work, though."

"If anything comes to you, would you shoot me a message?"

"I would, but I don't have your number," he said, his lips twitching with the hint of a grin.

"Oh, right." Addie pulled out her phone, found the contact entry he'd made the previous night, and sent him a quick text.

A sudden blast of bass-driven music had them both swiveling their heads to look across the street. Someone had just come out of Ripped, the supplement store between Betty's emporium and Hair Affair.

Trey made a face and shook his head. "I'm all for people expressing their own musical tastes, but at that volume, it's nothing but noise pollution."

Addie grimaced in agreement. "Yeah, I mean read the room, why don't you? The business owners on this street don't do that sort of thing."

"I get the feeling Lance, the guy who runs that place, doesn't really care about fitting in," Trey said. "I've got half a mind to report him for noise, but seeing as how I might have performances in my own store, I'm not sure I want to go down that road just yet. Plus, Lance just seems a little on the edge, if you know what I mean."

"Have you had a run-in with him?" Addie asked.

"No, not personally, but I know the type. He's the kind of dude who's always looking for a fight."

They both peered at Ripped for a moment, and then Trey said, "Well, I'd better get back at it." He pointed with his thumb over his shoulder into his retail space.

He disappeared inside his store, which was called Stargaze Acoustic by the temporary sign taped in the window, Addie noticed for the first time.

She mentally scolded herself. She'd been at Wild Rose for how many hours and was only just now noticing the name of the store next door. She was going to have to dial up her observation skills if she wanted to do her aunt any good. Fortunately, years of training as a scientist and many hours at the lab bench had honed her ability to observe, process information, and draw conclusions. She just needed to keep a cool head and tune into her logical side.

Shouldn't be hard. That was always one of Jeremy's big complaints about her, that she was too rational and not passionate enough.

Ugh, Jeremy. She scrunched her nose like she'd smelled something rotten.

Addie looked down at Lucky, who was still waiting expectantly.

"Let's get going," she said and set off toward the end of the block.

She intended to talk to Lisette, the irate owner of La Petite Patisserie. Addie wanted to understand what Lisette had been so upset about. Plus, maybe she'd seen or heard something that would help Addie find her aunt. It seemed like a good place to start.

AT THE CORNER, ADDIE WAITED until she was positive the traffic was clear for two blocks in every direction before crossing. But Lucky seemed like a dog used to being off leash, and he stuck close to her. Impressively, he wasn't even distracted by a squirrel in a tree next to Le Petite Patisserie. He went and sat in the shade under a table, as if knowing he wouldn't be able to follow her into the café.

When she spotted Lisette inside, Addie tried not to grimace. Squaring her shoulders, she pulled the door open and then waited at the counter until a man in a bowler hat paid for his croissant and coffee.

Lisette looked up with a pleasant expression, but then her red-tinted lips twisted when she recognized Addie. "What are you doing here?"

Addie decided not to lead with the part about her aunt being missing. Besides, the detective had said not to talk about the case.

"Why are you so ticked off at Kate?" Addie asked, seeing no reason to mince words.

Tossing up a hand and rolling her eyes, Lisette stomped over to a box that contained a few croissants, grabbed tongs, and continued filling the box from a tray.

"Your aunt had the gall to try to turn her store into a coffee shop," she practically spat out. "She didn't even talk to me first!"

"Sorry, but I'm confused," Addie said. "First of all, Wild Rose isn't a coffee shop. It has teas and herbal remedies. It doesn't serve coffee."

"But now she has tables. And chairs. And cinnamon twists. And free wi-fi."

"You think she's stealing business from you because she has four tables and a few food items?" Addie asked, truly perplexed.

Lisette dropped her tongs, and they landed on the counter with a clatter. "She didn't even have the decency to talk to me before she did it," she said through gritted teeth.

Out of the corner of her eye, Addie noticed someone standing in the doorway leading into the kitchen. It was a man, and he was giving her a wide-eyed look. He shook his head, drew his thumb across his neck, and then put the side of his index finger to his lips. He was obviously warning her to hush.

Seeing Addie's attention was elsewhere, Lisette narrowed her eyes. When she whirled around, the man stiffened guiltily.

"Babe, can you bring out more croissants?" she asked with slight snap in her voice, but sounding considerably calmer than when she spoke to Addie.

"Of course," he said. He shot one more wide-eyed look at Addie and shook his head before disappearing into the back.

Turning back to Addie, Lisette's eyes flashed. "You must be the one who sicced the police on me."

Addie's brows lifted.

"Oh yes, some detective called this morning." Lisette crossed her arms. "Something about your aunt. Having the police in here's going to be great for business," she said sarcastically. She turned away. "I need to get back to work."

What was that woman's problem? There was no reason to be that fired up over four little tables and a cinnamon twist or two in Wild Rose Teas and Apothecary. And from the looks of things, it wasn't Kate's shop that was keeping the business away from Lisette's café. Wild Rose wasn't even open at the moment, and La Petite Patisserie was empty except for one hipster twenty-something in the corner with his laptop.

Shaking her head and feeling more than a little irritated, Addie walked out with the intention of talking to Betty next. The long-time friend of Kate's would want to know about the robbery and her disappearance.

"C'mon, Lucky," Addie said. "Let's go to the emporium."

"Are you related to Kate James?" a male voice asked behind her.

She turned to find a man with brooding brown eyes standing on the sidewalk.

"Yes, I'm her niece, Addie."

He flicked a wary glance left and right and kept his body angled away from her, as if he didn't want observers to know they were talking.

"I may know something about what happened to your aunt," he said. "But we shouldn't talk here. Come to the office building across from the auto shop in ten minutes. Take the long way around the block."

Addie gave a little nod and turned away and started walking, trying to look nonchalant as a shot of adrenaline sent her pulse bumping. She was itching to find out who this man was and what he knew.

Chapter Six

WITH LUCKY AT HER HEEL, Addie passed Betty's emporium, the small supplement shop called Ripped that vibrated with metal music, and Hair Affair. Then she hung a left. Behind the salon was an office with a sign that read, "Chatterton and Bledsoe, Attorneys at Law," and then some empty retail space. The car shop the mysterious man had mentioned, called All Aces Auto Repair, was up ahead. It occupied the space behind La Petite Patisserie with an alley separating the businesses. A man with tattooed arms, a shaved head, and a dark-blond beard down to his chest was popping the hood of a mud-splashed SUV.

Even though the sun was out and the morning was pleasantly warm, Addie shivered as she peered around. There was something about this area that seemed different than the one just a block to the east of where Wild Rose was located. Maybe it was the empty-looking building across the street, or the fact that the only person in sight was the mechanic.

A plastic shopping bag tumbled by across the street, pushed along by the breeze, which only emphasized the forlorn, abandoned atmosphere. What would Chelsea say about the aura of this block?

If Addie could feel it, surely her sensitive friend would pick up on something, too.

Addie kept walking straight, past the auto shop and across the street to what she assumed was the office building the man had referred to. A faded sign in front of a three-story structure read, "Southgate Business Plaza." There was space at the bottom to list the businesses, but they were blank.

Slowing, she glanced around. Maybe she shouldn't be doing this alone. Her aunt had just been attacked and possibly abducted, and Addie had no idea who the man who'd spoken to her on the street was. She stopped halfway to the door of the entrance.

Just as she was thinking maybe she should wait for Chelsea, the door opened and the dark-eyed guy stood inside holding it.

"My name's Bennett Brooks," he said, once she'd stepped into the lobby. "Kate's come to my aid on more than one occasion, and I'd like to return the favor, if I can."

He gave her a small smile, which considerably warmed his brooding expression. That shift revealed he was actually a very handsome man, maybe early thirties, and with the smile and the dimples, he could have easily passed for John Legend's brother.

"Is it okay if my dog comes in, too?" Addie asked.

The question was a bit of a test, because if Bennett said no, she wasn't going to go inside. It didn't feel right to leave Lucky outside. Not here.

"Sure," he said, quirking his smile at the dog.

He waited, holding the door, while Addie and Lucky went into what seemed to pass as a lobby. Elevator doors stood to the right, a staircase straight ahead, and men's and women's restrooms to the left.

The linoleum was scratched and faded, and the walls really needed a new coat of paint. It wasn't dirty, but the tinted windows and tired interior gave it a dingy air.

"My office is up on the second floor. The elevator's out of commission," Bennett said, pointing to the stairs.

"What is it you do?" Addie asked as she followed him up.

"I've got a real estate license," he said over his shoulder. "But it's my P.I. license that's really the money maker."

"You're a private investigator?" Addie asked with surprise. "I wouldn't think a town like this would have a lot of need for that sort of service."

"Oh, you'd be surprised what goes on here," he said. "And apologies for asking you to take a circuitous route here. If a rumor got back to Stargaze P.D., it might not be good for your aunt's case."

"What do you mean?" Addie asked.

"The police don't appreciate the type of work I do. They wouldn't look kindly on you hiring a P.I.—or thinking you'd hired a P.I."

On the second floor, he turned right and went to a door marked only by a plaque labeled "Suite 202," where he punched in a code on the security pad.

Inside was a bare-bones office with a large desk that looked like it was from the eighties, a newer upholstered executive chair, a couple of folding chairs against one wall, and a tall bookshelf next to the chairs. A closed, unlabeled door took up the rest of the wall next to the shelving unit. On the opposite wall was a doorway to a darkened room that revealed a glimpse of a filing cabinet.

Bennett took one of the folding chairs and set it up in front of the desk. "You're welcome to sit," he said and then went around behind the desk.

The way he eased himself back in the seat and rocked slightly somehow gave the impression he spent a lot of time at this desk, despite the lack of items on the surface.

"Do you know where she is?" Addie asked, perching on the edge of the metal chair.

Lucky lay down at her feet, and she absently reached down to give his neck a scratch.

Bennett propped his elbows on the armrests and tented his fingers. "I don't know where she is now, but I saw her yesterday."

Her breath caught. "You did? When? Where? What was she doing?"

"When I came into the office at seven fifteen, she was headed south on foot." He pointed to the right.

"What's south of here?"

He tilted his head and pressed his lips together for a moment. "It's the area beyond the empty building you walked past to get here. It's a bit, well, I guess you'd say it's not the part of town where tourists would want to stroll around."

Addie wrapped her arms around her ribs, remembering the eerie sense she'd gotten as she'd walked down the block he was talking about.

"What's out there?" she pressed.

"There's a homeless shelter. Apartment buildings. Warehouses. A self-storage lot. A long-haul truck fleet is based over there."

Something pinged in Addie's memory.

"Is the soup kitchen over there? She volunteers regularly."

He nodded. "It is."

"Well, how did she look? Was she hurrying? Did she seem worried?"

"She walked with purpose, but she wasn't in a rush."

Addie frowned and peered down at the floor, thinking. "I wonder why she walked instead of taking her car. Seven fifteen in the morning seems awfully early to be volunteering. Wild Rose opens at nine on weekdays. It sounds like she probably didn't open the store at all yesterday."

"I went to get coffee at La Petite Patisserie at nine thirty on the dot, and Wild Rose still had the closed sign in the door. I'd reckon you're right."

From the way he talked, Addie got the impression Bennett was the type of person who tended followed the same schedule every day and always took note of details like the time. She could appreciate such a quality. And, of course, it made sense for a P.I. to be so alert and aware.

She tilted her gaze up at him. "What do you think happened to her? You said you thought you might know."

He bit his lower lip, regarding her silently for a long moment. His expression was more grimace than smile, but it brought out a dimple on his left cheek. With his straight and white teeth, perfect skin, and eyes with depth, he was a very good-looking man. Could Kate have been involved with him? Unlikely. He was probably at least twenty years younger than her, and Kate wasn't the type to have flings with much younger men. As far as Addie knew, her aunt wasn't the type to have flings, period.

"Has your aunt ever talked to you about a . . . unique population in Stargaze?" he asked.

Unique population? There were a lot of really outdoorsy people in the town, but there was nothing special about that in an area that had lots of trails, a lake, and a ski resort nearby. Seasonal workers weren't particularly unique, either. Besides, Addie got the

impression he meant something much more unusual than anything
that came to her mind.

"No idea what you're talking about," Addie said with a shake of her
head.

"There's a certain community, a sort of sub-culture here, one that
tries to keep a very low profile," he said, watching her carefully.
"They're afflicted with—actually, if you don't already know about
them, I shouldn't say anything further."

"What, is there a leper colony in Stargaze?" she asked in a joking
tone.

He didn't even crack a smile. Addie's insides tensed.

"You've got to tell me," she said. "If it has something to do with my
aunt, I really, really need to know."

"I know you and Kate are close, and the only reason I brought it
up was that I'd thought maybe your aunt had . . . introduced you,"
he said, the corners of his mouth turning down slightly. "They're
protective of their own. It'd be dangerous for me to tell you, if you
aren't already on the inside."

This man knew something that might lead to Kate, Addie was
positive of it.

"On the inside of what? Please, Bennett," she said, clasping her
hands tightly in her lap. A lump started to form in her throat. "I'm
afraid she might be badly hurt. Or even dead. I—I shouldn't be
telling you this because it's still under investigation, but you already
seem to know that the police are involved, anyway. Last night I came
downstairs and found her unconscious."

She described what had happened and how Kate had seemingly
disappeared into thin air. A tear slipped down Addie's cheek.
She tried to furtively brush it away—she hated getting emotional,
especially in front of someone she barely knew—but of course he

saw. He pulled out a drawer and came up with a tissue, which he passed to her.

"Thanks," she said, bunching it in her fist.

"I think Kate was helping this group," he said quietly. He leaned forward, resting his forearms on the desk, and peered at her intently. "I think she may have been involved with them for some time."

"And you think they hurt her?"

He squinted, casting his gaze up to a corner of the room.

"No," he said after a moment. "I don't think they would attack her. They rely quite a lot on their—uh, their allies. But she could have been hurt by accident."

Addie's heart dropped.

"It looked like a robbery, though, not an accident," she said. Her voice dropped to a trembling whisper. "Do you think she could be dead?"

His eyes locked on hers again. "I refuse to go there."

His resolve made her feel a lot better and brought her back from the edge of tears.

"What should I do? Where do I look for her?" Addie asked. "I don't know this town as well as you and the other locals. And not having a clear picture of who she's involved with puts me at a huge disadvantage."

She hoped he'd see the light and tell her the secret, but he didn't bite.

"You said you tried calling her all day and got no answer?" he asked.

She nodded.

"I'm going to see if I can track down the location of her phone." He reached over to his open laptop and pressed the power button on the side.

Straightening, Addie perked up. "You can do that? I thought only the police could do that. Or, maybe not even the police. More like the FBI."

His lips twitched, and his lids lowered partway as he cast her a conspiratorial glance. "I've got a few tricks up my sleeve."

"I like the sound of that," Addie said. "I tried calling the police for an update this morning. So far, Detective McCann has blown me off. I'm sure they're busy, but . . . actually, you know what? This is Stargaze. I bet they're not that busy. Yeah, she's just blowing me off."

Bennett had grimaced at the mention of McCann's name. "I wouldn't expect them to be forthcoming with you."

Remembering how the detective seemed to disapprove of Kate, Addie tilted her head. "Why's that?"

"They're not too stoked about the group I mentioned. They're not fans of anyone who helps them, either."

"Really," Addie said slowly. "So, you're saying the police are aware of the, uh, not-lepers in Stargaze?"

He nodded.

She leaned back in her chair. "Huh. Well. I guess I'll have to rely on you to be my investigative ally." Giving him a direct look, she silently challenged him to refuse.

But he didn't seem concerned about getting drawn into her amateur investigation. He was typing on his laptop, and if anything, he seemed to be hitting the keys with enthusiasm.

"Yep," he said. "I want to help Kate, if I can."

"You mentioned she did something for you," Addie said. "Mind if I ask what it was?"

"She makes custom-formulated remedies for me," he said without looking up. His tone said he wasn't interested in discussing details.

Fair enough. Kate wasn't a doctor, but her clients still deserved confidentiality. Addie couldn't help one more attempt at getting him to reveal the other secret, though.

"I'm really glad to have run into you," Addie said. "But it would make things a heck of a lot easier if you'd just tell me about the people Kate's involved with."

Bennett stopped typing and shook his head firmly. "No can do. It'd be dangerous for you to start poking that bear. Leave that part to me. I'm going to look into some things." He pushed a pad and pencil across the desk. "Write down your number so I can get a hold of you."

Addie printed her phone number in neat block text.

"Day or night, don't hesitate to call if you learn anything," she said.

"You'll be the first to know, I promise," he said with a confident assurance that made Addie feel more at ease than she had all morning.

She stood, and he rose and came around the desk to see her to the door. Lucky popped up to go, too.

"I'll talk to you soon, Addie," he said and closed his office door as she walked toward the stairs.

Back out in the sunshine, Addie moved with a purposeful stride.

It felt good to have someone on her side, someone who might actually have a lead on where Kate could be. Who better than a P.I. to help?

It was extremely unfortunate he wouldn't give her more details about the mysterious group Kate had gotten mixed up with, but he'd made one thing clear: the police weren't going to be especially motivated to solve her aunt's case.

With or without the police, Addie knew one thing for certain. She wasn't going to give up until she found her aunt—dead or alive. And the person who attacked Kate was probably the best place to start.

Chapter Seven

ADDIE AND LUCKY HEADED BACK toward Pine Avenue, where Wild Rose Teas and Apothecary was located, and with no desire to tangle with Lisette again, Addie sped up when she passed La Petite Patisserie. Glimpsing Betty inside the emporium, Addie waved though the window, and the mystic beckoned her inside and let out a delighted little laugh when Addie introduced Lucky.

"Betty," Addie said, turning serious. "I need to tell you about what happened last night."

She recounted the story, which she'd gotten pretty practiced at by that point, having described it all to the police and Detective McCann several times and then Bennett as well.

Betty's hand flew to her mouth when Addie got to the part about finding her aunt on the floor. The mystic gasped in distress and sank heavily onto the easy chair as Addie described coming back into the shop and finding her aunt gone.

"Oh, no, poor Kate," Betty said, shaking her head and fluttering her long fake lashes. She touched her throat and then pointed to the mug at the end of the table with the coffee and tea spread. "Could you hand me my tea, dearie? The shock of this terrible news has made my mouth go dry."

Addie reached for the mug, and the steeping tea ball reminded her of one of the other odd things that had happened the previous night. After handing it to Betty, who was fanning her flushed face, Addie sat down on the ottoman.

"Remember when I was a kid and you taught me the little ritual for tea-leaf reading?" she mused, just to make a bit of conversation while Betty collected herself.

The older woman nodded. "Tasseomancy. Sometimes called tasseography. Yes, I remember." Her eyes sharpened on Addie. "Why do you ask?"

Addie blinked. She really hadn't wanted to get into the strange episode with the vision in the tea leaves.

She waved a hand. "Oh, no reason, really."

"Betty knows when a person is dancing around the truth. Especially when it's something like this." The mystic's voice had deepened, and her gaze was so intense Addie wanted to squirm. "Tell me, dearie."

The words were kind, but the tone left no room for argument or denial.

Swallowing hard, Addie ran a hand over the goosebumps that had risen on her arm.

"I, uh, looked into the tea leaves last night," she said. "It was after Aunt Kate disappeared, and I couldn't sleep. I did what you taught me all those years ago. Then things took a strange turn."

She quickly described seeing little detailed pictures in the herbs and the unsettling physical sensations she'd experienced. Then she pulled out her phone.

"I took a picture of the cup," she said. "I'm not even sure why I did it."

Betty leaned forward and barely gave the picture a glance before closing her hand around Addie's wrist.

"The leaves were telling you something," Betty said. "What exactly were you thinking of as you drank the tea?"

"Kate. I was missing her. Worrying about her and wondering who hurt her and where she was."

Betty pressed her pink-lipsticked mouth into a thin line, her eyes sparking. "Addie, dearie, it sounds as though you have the gift."

Addie pulled back, scrunching her nose. "What? No. This isn't a gift. I'm not like you. It was just, I don't know, a product of stress, exhaustion, and maybe something in the tea. Besides, there's something much more important I wanted to talk about. What do you know about the secret community that operates somewhere west of here? They're possibly afflicted with a disease?"

The mystic's expression shifted from concerned to closed-off, the wrinkles around her eyes deepening. "What do you mean?"

"A friend of Kate's thought they might have something to do with what happened to her," Addie said, watching Betty's face carefully. "You know what I'm talking about, don't you?"

"What, exactly, did this friend tell you?" Betty asked, her tone sharpening.

It occurred to Addie to try and overstate what Bennett had revealed to make it sound like she knew a lot more than she did in an attempt to get Betty to speak freely. But Addie suspected the mystic couldn't be fooled that way.

"He didn't reveal much," Addie admitted. "Only that he'd seen Kate walking west yesterday morning, this group he mentioned is somewhere in that direction, and he knows she's been mixed up with them. He said they consider her a friend, but he also made them sound potentially dangerous."

Betty made a displeased humming noise at the back of her throat.

Addie spread her hands in a pleading gesture. "You know about them, too. I can see that. Please, don't keep me in the dark."

"This friend of Kate's should not have revealed what he did," Betty said.

"Maybe so, but he also told me not to expect much enthusiasm from the police in solving Kate's case," Addie said, starting to lose hope that Betty would disclose anything helpful. "That means I'm going to have to look into it myself. You and my aunt have been close for years, and I can't believe you would withhold information that might help me—that would help *her*."

"But you do have help, dearie," Betty said. She gestured at Addie's phone.

"What, the tea leaves?" Addie's tone became heated, but she couldn't hide her frustration. "Are you serious?"

"Gravely serious. The leaves have given you some answers already. Don't turn away from them."

Gripping her phone hard, Addie stood. She'd had enough of the mystical mumbo jumbo.

"I'm sorry, Betty, but that's ridiculous," Addie said. She shoved her phone in her back pocket. "If no one's going to tell me what's going on, I guess I'll just have to dig into it myself."

The mystic struggled to her feet as Addie turned toward the door. Lucky hopped up to follow her.

"Wait, Addie, you must listen to me," Betty said.

"I'm sorry, but if you're not going to tell me the truth, I need to go," Addie said, and left.

She wheeled around, walked out, and nearly ran into someone.

Chelsea squealed in surprise. "I tried to call, but when you didn't pick up, I figured I'd just come looking for you," she said. Then she took in Addie's agitation. "What's wrong? Did you get news about your aunt?"

"No. Sort of. I don't know," Addie said, running a hand over her hair to smooth back stray strands.

"Why don't we grab a bite and you can tell me what's going on, hon?" Chelsea suggested.

Addie checked her phone and discovered it was nearly noon. The morning had flown by, and her stomach was starting to feel hollow with hunger. "Okay, that's a good idea."

Bending over and placing her hands on her knees, Chelsea looked down at Lucky. "Hey, who's this little cutie?"

"Oh, that's Lucky," Addie said, her tone softening. "He showed up at the shop this morning, and he insisted on coming with me."

He wagged at the sound of his name.

Chelsea straightened. "He insisted?" She chuckled.

"Yeah, he threw a fit when I tried to leave him behind," Addie said. "I don't know who he belongs to, and I figured I could ask around. I mentioned him to Trey, but—oh, shoot. I actually forgot to ask everyone else I've talked to." She shook her head, feeling deflated. The boost she'd felt after talking to Bennett seemed to have dissipated. "I'm kind of failing on all fronts this morning, I feel like."

"Let's get some food, and you'll feel better," Chelsea said. She pointed down the street. "I think you'll like the Grinning Catfish Brewery. Plus, I wouldn't mind running into Pete, one of the owners. We flirted a little, and I've been hoping he'll ask me out."

Addie nodded. "Sure."

They walked the short distance to the brewery, and Lucky lay down on the small patch of grass under a tree at the edge of the restaurant's parking lot to wait.

Addie and Chelsea got a table near the window, giving them a view of Hair Affair, which was kitty-corner to the pub and the bookstore directly across the street. Addie avoided looking at the emporium. It was too bad things had gotten tense with Betty and they'd parted on an unpleasant note, but Addie needed real information. Facts. Not crystal-ball nonsense. Certainly not someone telling her that soggy tea leaves were the answer.

A guy in his mid-twenties with sparkling tawny-brown eyes and a small piercing in one ear came to take their order. He gave Chelsea a broad grin, his eyes lingering on her a little longer than necessary.

"Hi, Pete," Chelsea said, giving him a sunny smile. "This is Addie James. She's Kate's niece."

He nodded at Addie. "Nice to meet you. What can I get started for you?"

She and Chelsea ordered iced tea and burgers, and the shot of caffeine helped perk Addie up a bit. She told Chelsea about all the events of the morning, from Lucky's appearance to the visit to La Petite Patisserie, then running into Bennett, and finally her exchange with Betty. Well, Addie recounted everything except the tea-leaf incident and Betty's insistence that Addie had a "gift." She wasn't in the mood to talk about that.

"Please tell me you know about the secret society in the west part of town," Addie said and then took a big bite of hamburger. The patty was made in-house, and it was perfectly cooked and seasoned.

Chelsea squinted and then shook her head slowly. "I've heard some rumors about some odd happenings in that area. There was a string of tourists disappearing, too."

Addie stopped chewing and then swallowed. "Disappearances? Were people abducted?" Her heart dropped as she imagined Kate falling victim to the same fate.

"I'm not sure. I don't think the cases were resolved. But I was a teenager when it happened and didn't pay a ton of attention other than staying away from that area of town. It was the summer you didn't visit, remember?"

"Vaguely. That was the year Dad and Aunt Kate got into a disagreement and my parents wouldn't let me come here," Addie said. "Were the people ever found?"

Chelsea shrugged. "I'm not sure. Come to think of it, I'm not sure I ever heard anything more about it. But I was a kid with other things on my mind."

"But you don't know what I'm talking about? You don't know anything about this supposed community?"

"No," Chelsea said. "I swear I'd tell you if I did."

Addie sighed. "I guess I'm just going to have to look into it myself."

"But it sounds like they're friends of Kate's and this Bennett guy knows about them. So maybe for now we could let him look into that, like he said. And I was thinking we should make a suspect list." Chelsea reached into her knit cross-body bag and whipped out a purple gel pen and notebook with a sparkly cover.

Addie still intended to look into what was west of the empty building, but if she was serious about investigating, and she absolutely was, a suspect list sounded like a good starting point for organizing her investigation. If she could find the person who attacked Kate, he or she might lead Addie to where her aunt was.

"Okay, let's start with what we know," Chelsea said, flipping to a fresh page. "There's one person who's pretty darn ticked off at Kate."

"Lisette," they said at the same time in low tones.

"You really think she's capable of hurting someone, though?" Addie asked. "She's so tiny and thin. I really don't think she could overpower Kate."

Chelsea went still for a moment and then looked up. She seemed hesitant to speak but finally said, "She's got a temper."

"Obviously, but would she get physical?"

Chelsea nodded, her blue eyes serious.

"You've seen this, I take it?" Addie asked.

Another nod. Chelsea hunched over, seeming uncomfortable all of a sudden.

"What happened?"

"She got angry and . . . threw things," Chelsea said reluctantly.

Addie's brows rose. "Okay. I guess she belongs on the list."

She still had her doubts, though. Lisette was a small woman, and even in a rage, Addie just couldn't see it.

"We need to figure out if she has an alibi for last night," Chelsea said.

"You're right." Addie slumped. "But I really, really don't want to have to talk to her again."

"No kidding, me neither. Hey, how about if we ask her husband instead? He usually mans the café alone for a while in the afternoon."

"Good plan. Let's do that after lunch."

"Who else goes on the list?" Chelsea asked.

Addie shrugged. "What about that guy who delivered our pizza? You said he served time for robbery, and I think he was eyeing the cash register when I was paying him for our pizza. Maybe he came back to rob the place."

"Sure, that's possible. Enzo," Chelsea said and added the name in curly script. "We'll check his alibi, too. Do you think Zelda is a suspect?"

"Hmm. Maybe a person of interest," Addie said. "I'd really like to know why she seemed irritated when I mentioned my aunt. They've been neighbors for years. Not best friends by any means, but as far as I know, they've always been on good terms."

"Okay, I'll put her down for questioning." Chelsea drew a line down the middle of the page to make a second column, where she wrote Zelda's name. "That seems like plenty for us to do for now."

They finished eating and split the bill. Addie watched with a little grin as Chelsea wrote her name and phone number on a slip of paper torn from her notebook, folded it, and wrote Pete's name on the top.

"I know this is so seventh-grade," Chelsea said, her cheeks pinking faintly. "But the man isn't taking the hint."

They got up and walked outside.

Addie had kept a little piece of hamburger wrapped in a napkin, which she fed to an eager Lucky.

"I need to get you some proper dog food later," she said. Rising, she turned to Chelsea and then glanced down the street. "Think it's safe to go to La Petite Patisserie?"

They peered toward the café together.

"We might as well find out," Chelsea said.

The three of them walked back the way they'd come, passing Hair Affair. Addie happened to glance across the street, and her heart leapt into her throat when she saw someone peering in the window of Wild Rose Teas and Apothecary—a woman who looked just like Aunt Kate from the back. But then the woman turned, and it was clearly someone else.

"That's Georgia, Lance's girlfriend," Chelsea said. "He's the one that owns this place." She tipped her head at Ripped, the store they were in front of.

The supplement shop was dark, even though it was past the opening time posted in the window.

Addie watched as Georgia knocked on the door of Wild Rose, even though the sign read "closed." Then she turned and looked up and down the street, biting at her thumbnail.

If Kate didn't show up soon, Addie thought she might open the store for a few hours at some point, just to give the regulars a chance to come in for the herbal remedies or tea. She'd worked at Wild Rose enough over the years to know how to help people find what they needed and ring up purchases.

She and Chelsea reached the café, and to Addie's great relief, Lisette was nowhere in sight. A man was inside wiping off tables.

Chelsea pulled the door open. "Put your detective hat on," she whispered to Addie.

The man inside looked up. "I remember you from earlier," he said to Addie with a hint of an Indian accent.

"Um, yeah," she said, her gaze flicking to the doorway leading into the kitchen in back. "Is Lisette around?"

He shook his head. "She's meeting with the accountant."

"Actually, that's good," Addie said, relieved. "We wanted to talk to you."

"Oh, okay. I'm Viraj Kumar, by the way. Lisette's husband," he said. He came forward and stuck out his hand. "Most people call me Raj."

Flashing a grin, he seemed a lot more relaxed than earlier that morning. He moved in an easy way that made Addie think he might have been a serious athlete at some point. But his slight paunch indicated he probably wasn't terribly active these days. Or maybe he just overindulged in his wife's goodies. It would be hard not to. Even though Lisette was kind of a nightmare, her pastries looked absolutely exquisite.

"Addie James," she introduced herself and shook his hand. "And this is Chelsea Spring, whom I imagine your wife may have already mentioned."

Raj gave Chelsea a wry nod, his eyebrows lifting a bit.

Addie took a deep breath to try to calm her nerves. She wasn't used to interrogating people. It seemed weird to jump right in, but she wasn't sure how else to get to the point. Plus, she wanted to get this over with before Lisette returned. "This may sound like a weird question, but do you know where your wife was between eleven and midnight last night?"

He rocked back on his heels and crossed his arms, his smile fading.

"At home," he said.

"With you?" Chelsea asked.

"Yeah." He shrugged. "I'd gone to bed, and she stayed up to do some paperwork."

Addie exchanged a glance with Chelsea.

"So, you were asleep at that time?" Addie asked.

"I guess so," he said. His eyes narrowed. "Does this have something to do with why that detective wanted to talk to Lisette?"

"Why is Lisette so angry with Kate?" Addie asked, ignoring his question.

Raj rubbed at the back of his neck. "Oh, Liz doesn't mean anything by it. She's just stressed because the café isn't taking off as well as she'd hoped."

"She seemed awfully worked up, though," Addie pressed. "Does she really think Kate is sabotaging the café by setting up a couple of tables in Wild Rose?"

Chelsea had remained quiet, standing a half step behind Addie.

"I know, it seems a little unreasonable," Raj said apologetically. His lips pinched, and he was obviously uncomfortable with the direction the conversation was going. "She just has a bit of a, you know, short fuse."

"It's a *lot* more than just a short fuse," Chelsea said quietly.

Addie turned to see that her friend was slightly pale and had her arms folded tightly.

Raj's gaze shifted to Chelsea. "So, you've seen the—the things she does when she loses her temper?" he asked, his voice so low it was nearly a whisper.

Chelsea gave a tiny nod.

Confused, Addie looked back and forth between the two of them. "What are you talking about? Someone please fill me in."

"I didn't want to tell you because I know how you feel about these kinds of things," Chelsea said.

Addie frowned. "What kinds of things?"

"When Liz gets really mad, she, well . . ." Raj trailed off and then cleared his throat. "She throws things."

"Okay," Addie said slowly. She turned to Chelsea. "It sounds like she needs some anger-management therapy, but why wouldn't you want to tell me about this?"

"Because," Chelsea said. "Lisette throws things with her mind."

Chapter Eight

FOR A FEW SECONDS, ADDIE stared at Chelsea and then at Raj. Was this some kind of prank? Neither of them looked like they were joking.

"Did I really hear you correctly?" Addie asked incredulously. "Lisette *throws* things with her *mind?*"

She loved Chelsea, but this was one of those times she veered off into a place Addie had a hard time following. It wasn't the first time this had happened in the course of their friendship. But Addie had always been willing to put up with a few quirks because she genuinely loved Chels and they had such a long history together.

Addie squinted at Raj. He didn't seem like the type to be into woo-woo nonsense, but she'd only just met him.

She turned to Chelsea. "You've seen Lisette do this?" Addie asked.

"It's one of the reasons she hated me so much when we were younger," Chelsea said. "I saw her lose control. I knew her secret. It humiliated her, and she was scared I'd tell someone that she had telekinetic abilities."

Giving her head a little shake, Addie pictured her aunt lying motionless on the tea shop floor. Had Lisette come in to confront

Kate and used telekinesis to fling the heavy cash register at her, causing her to stumble into the counter and hit her head? Addie had been sure there was no way Lisette could physically overpower Kate, but . . .

Addie wasn't quite ready to accept the paranormal bit, but she couldn't strike Lisette from the suspect list because Raj couldn't truly confirm she'd been home at the time Kate was attacked. Lisette's alibi was weak.

Motion at the back of the café pulled Addie from her thoughts. Someone was standing there in the kitchen doorway.

Addie's stomach plummeted. It was Lisette.

She strode forward, her expression clouding.

"What are you doing here?" she demanded.

"Did you hurt my aunt?" Addie asked. "Did you attack her in her shop last night?"

Lisette's glance flicked to Chelsea and then shifted back to Addie.

"What do you think you're doing, playing detective? I was at home all night, for your information." Lisette's eyes tightened, and her jaw clenched. Through gritted teeth, she said, "Leave now, or I'll file a report for harassment with the police."

Addie's anger flared, but Chelsea was pulling her toward the door and out to the sidewalk.

"C'mon," Chelsea said. "We don't need to start a fight."

"Maybe if she attacked us, the police would take her seriously as a suspect," Addie said, glaring over her shoulder at the café, where it looked like Raj was trying to calm his wife. "But as far as I'm concerned, Lisette is still very much on our list."

Lucky trotted with them across the street, and Addie tried to shake off her annoyance.

Once they'd made it to the corner, Addie stopped and blasted out a breath. "What do we do now? Do we tell the police that Lisette's alibi sucks and she has a bad temper?"

She certainly wasn't going to call Detective McCann and say that Lisette was a violent telekinetic.

"You don't believe me, do you?" Chelsea asked.

"About the . . ." Addie trailed off. She softened her expression and met her friend's gaze. "Look, it's not that I think you're lying. It's just really hard for me to wrap my head around something like that."

Chelsea nodded. "Yeah, I knew it would be." She sighed. "I hate to say that Lisette was right about something, but I don't think the authorities will appreciate us poking around on our own, so I don't think we should report her to the police."

"You're right, we need something a lot more solid before we do that," Addie said. "And Chelsea, it's not that I don't believe you. It's just the kind of thing I'd need to see for myself, you know? And it doesn't mean I'm not extremely grateful for what you're doing."

Her friend brightened. "I know. I'm so glad you're back in town."

"Me too. But you have to tell me if I'm keeping you from work. I appreciate what you're doing, but I really don't expect you to drop everything for me."

Chelsea shook her head, her blond waves tumbling around her shoulders. "Nah, I've got Lang full-time and another part-time employee to take care of the boutique. I don't need to be there. I just like to go in to open the store in the mornings because it gives me a sense of purpose and it's fun to help customers."

Chelsea had always been into fashion, and the boutique was a dream of hers, even though she didn't need the income. It wasn't something Chelsea liked to talk about, but she was quite a wealthy young woman. Her father, with whom she'd had a very rocky relationship, had died a few years back, leaving Chelsea a small fortune. She was the sole heir because her parents had divorced long ago and her mother had taken off when Chelsea was a little girl. Even though she'd never wanted for anything material, Addie knew Chelsea's childhood had plenty of sadness and difficulty.

"Well, that guy Enzo is next on our list," Addie said. "Should we check out the pizza place to see if he's there?"

"Sure, let's go," Chelsea said.

They were quiet on the walk to the next street over, where Slice of Pie was located. Addie couldn't help feeling guilty because her reaction to Lisette's supposed telekinesis had obviously hurt Chelsea's feelings. Even though she was nearly always sunshine and smiles, Addie knew her friend sometimes used her disposition to hide deeper hurt. It was a coping mechanism learned in childhood during the years she'd had to survive life with a volatile father and no mother.

Addie had spent some time around Chelsea's father during the many summer weeks in Stargaze over the years and remembered him as a moody, sometimes angry man who seemed overly strict with his daughter. It struck Addie that Lisette's temper might be triggering some difficult memories for Chelsea.

"Hey, did Lisette hurt you? Physically, I mean?" Addie asked softly.

"She tried to. When I was elected cheer captain over her in middle school, she waited for me after cheerleading practice and basically ambushed me, accusing me of bribing the other girls to vote for me," Chelsea said. "That was another ongoing thing between us. Her family struggled, and she was really jealous that I had money. She seemed to think that money and popularity meant I could pay people to do what I wanted and that I never had any problems."

"So, was that the time you learned about her telekinesis?" Addie asked, forcing herself to say the word without stumbling.

Chelsea gave a little sigh and nodded. "We were alone in the gym. There were some folding chairs stacked against the wall. She hurled one at me, and it missed me by a hair. It scared me to death. I ran out of there as fast as I could. She came after me, and I think she was trying to apologize, but it came out more of a threat. She was really afraid that everyone would find out she was a freak, in her words."

"Wow. All this time, I knew she was your nemesis, but I didn't really understand how deep it ran."

"Yeah, and it hasn't ended," Chelsea said with a humorless laugh. "She's still angry that I ended up getting the retail space she wanted, even though she couldn't afford it."

Addie pursed her lips with disapproval. "Sounds like she's the type of person who tends to blame others for her problems."

"She does that sometimes," Chelsea said. "But she had a really rough time growing up, and I think she has a lot of scars."

"You're a lot more understanding than I would be."

"Eh, I didn't have the easiest childhood either, so I guess I can't help having some empathy."

They'd reached Slice of Pie, and like the good boy he'd been all day, Lucky went to sit under one of the tables on the sidewalk. Addie opened the door, and a chime announced their arrival. A man with a shining bald head and a thick moustache was rolling out a circle of dough on the stainless-steel work surface behind the counter.

"Hello there, Chelsea," he said with an East Coast accent, his eyes twinkling. "How's the boutique?"

"Hey, Antonio," Chelsea greeted him with a grin. "It's going really well, thanks for asking. How is business here?"

"Steady as always. It's a little early for dinner, but I can start a pie for you, if you'd like," he said.

"Oh, we're not here for pizza," Chelsea said. "We had one last night, and it was delicious, though. Is Enzo around?"

Antonio arched a bushy brow, clearly surprised. "You want to see my nephew?"

"Just to ask him a couple of questions," Addie jumped in. "I'm Addie James, by the way."

"Ah, yes, Kate's niece. I remember you from summers past. Nice to see you." Antonio brushed his hands together, raising a little cloud of flour. "Enzo's in the back unpacking some boxes. I'll go get him."

A moment later, Antonio and his nephew emerged. A broad smile spread over Enzo's face when he caught sight of Addie and Chelsea, and he sauntered around the counter to where they waited.

"Well, well, well," he drawled. "Look who's come asking for me."

"Behave yourself," Antonio said to his nephew in a warning tone.

Enzo, with his back turned to the older man, rolled his eyes.

"I've gotta work until ten, but after that, you ladies wanna hang?" he asked.

Addie ground her teeth in irritation, but before she could snap at Enzo, Chelsea jumped in with a smile.

"Thanks for the invite, but unfortunately we've got plans," Chelsea said. "But we were wondering what you were up to last night between eleven and twelve?"

He cocked his head. "Uh, I was at Uncle Tony's playing video games."

"Was Antonio with you?" Chelsea asked.

Enzo shook his head. "He had poker night with his buddies."

"Do you have proof?" Addie blurted.

"Huh?" Enzo frowned in confusion.

Addie tried to rein in her impatience. "Proof of where you were last night."

He pulled out his phone. "I've gotta pic of myself I posted."

He thumbed the screen for a minute and then held out the phone. It displayed a selfie of Enzo sitting on a sofa, holding up a bottle of beer, and grinning. The timestamp was a quarter past eleven.

It wasn't definitive proof. He could have snapped the picture and then left. Antonio's apartment was located on the second floor of the building they were standing in, and it would have taken Enzo only a minute or two to get to Wild Rose.

"You didn't go anywhere after that picture was taken?" Chelsea asked.

Enzo lowered his phone. "Nuh uh. I gamed and drank and fell asleep on the couch. Hey, what's this about, anyway?"

Chelsea gave a charming little laugh and shrugged. "Oh, just interested in how you like to spend your free time." She grabbed Addie's arm and pulled her toward the door. "See you later."

"Wait, don't go. I got some free time I could spend with you," Enzo called after them. "I'm on break in ten minutes!"

Outside, Chelsea tugged Addie away from Slice of Pie, walking quickly.

"What's with the quick exit?" Addie asked, confused.

Chelsea looked over her shoulder. "Did you see that?"

"What?"

"On his phone. He had an email open before he flipped to the pic. Confirmation for a one-way plane ticket purchased this afternoon. Final destination New York."

Addie skidded to a halt. "Wait, what? Didn't you tell me he wanted to get back there but didn't have the money? And how the heck did you even see that?"

Chelsea nodded, also stopping. "He had his phone tipped toward me. How do you suppose he suddenly has enough cash for a flight?"

Lucky stood between them, looking up as if following the conversation.

The image of the overturned, empty cash register flashed through Addie's mind. "You really think he robbed Wild Rose last night and did . . . *that* to Aunt Kate?"

Chelsea frowned. "I mean, logically it fits together. But honestly, I don't think he'd be that good a liar. He wasn't nervous at all when we just questioned him."

"Maybe that's because he's a hardened criminal," Addie suggested.

"But not a smart one. He got caught and thrown in jail."

Addie licked her lips. "Did his, uh, aura tell you anything helpful?"

"No, nothing jumped out at me," Chelsea said.

"I don't know," Addie said. "I tend to agree with your instinct. He doesn't seem too bright, and I don't think he's crafty, either. But there's motive. His alibi is poor, so there's opportunity. And though he's not a big guy, he's really muscular, so there's means."

Chelsea raised her brows. "Look at you, using crime-show words."

Addie cracked a small smile that quickly faded. "I don't think we can eliminate him from the suspect list yet."

"You're probably right."

"On the TV shows, it seems like alibis are a lot more cut and dried," Addie said. "I'd hoped we'd have some answers by now, but it all still seems up in the air. I just really want to find Kate."

Her phone vibrated in her pocket. She pulled it out and answered. "Hello?"

"Hi, Addie. It's Bennett Brooks. I've been doing some tracking on Kate's phone, and it looks like it was either turned off or the battery died this morning."

Addie straightened, pressing the phone harder to her ear. "But were you able to see a location before that happened?"

"Yes," he said. "The last active location appears to be right next door to Wild Rose."

"Zelda's antique shop?"

"Yep."

How had Kate's phone ended up there?

"Huh. That . . . wasn't what I expected," Addie said. "My friend and I are nearby, so we'll go there now. Thank you so much for the info. I'll let you know what we find out."

"Sure thing. Talk to you soon."

Addie disconnected and turned to Chelsea.

"Let's go find out if we'll be moving Zelda from person of interest to suspect."

Chapter Nine

WHEN THEY REACHED ZELDA'S A to Z Antiques, there was a white-haired man talking to the owner, so Addie peered into the jewelry in the cases as she sidled closer.

Chelsea was going to look around for anything suspicious—including Kate's phone—while Addie spoke to Zelda. Addie had never been one to try to listen in on other people's conversations, but this situation had her stepping outside of her usual reserved demeanor.

Her eavesdropping revealed the man was looking for an antique watch for his wife. Clearly nothing to do with the robbery or Kate's disappearance.

Zelda showed the man where the collection of antique watches was located, and when she looked up, she stiffened at the sight of Addie.

"Hello," Zelda said. "Do you need help with something?"

Though she wasn't a young woman, she was large—close to six feet and solidly built. Could she overtake Kate? Definitely. Especially if she didn't see the attack coming.

"Hello, Zelda," Addie said. "I wanted to ask you about something that's been nagging at me. You seemed agitated when I brought up my aunt yesterday. Are you and Kate having problems?"

Zelda's gaze skipped away, roving around the shop. "Problems? No. No problems."

With a glance at the man still perusing the antique watches, Addie beckoned to Zelda. "Why don't we talk over there?" She pointed to the checkout counter.

The corners of the older woman's mouth turned down, but she nodded and followed Addie. They stood at one end of the counter.

"You and Aunt Kate have always been on good terms," Addie said. "But that's obviously changed lately."

"Nope. Everything's fine." She crossed her arms.

Addie blinked. What was she supposed to do with an uncooperative suspect? Change tacks.

"Well, there's another reason I wanted to talk to you," Addie said. "I think my aunt left her phone here. Have you seen it?"

"No," Zelda said, but her face had paled and one eye twitched.

"Are you sure? Maybe I could just take a look around."

"If you're not buying anything, you don't need to be here."

That made Addie pause again. She'd never known Zelda to be this abrupt and defensive. Addie's eyes flicked past Zelda's shoulder to Chelsea, who'd been slowly moving closer.

"Zelda," Addie said, softening her tone as much as she could. "We've known each other for years. And I have to tell you, I have information that indicates Kate's phone was left here. Now, she may have set it down and you might not have even known it. But I'd really appreciate it if you'd let me look. You probably noticed Wild Rose was closed all day yesterday and it's still closed today. That's because she's *missing*. She might be hurt. Aren't you even a little concerned about her?"

"Customers only." Zelda tugged at the end of her braid in an agitated gesture. "No loitering. That's the rule."

Frowning, Addie shook her head in confusion. Why was Zelda acting so strangely? Her gaze slipped past the older woman to a colorful bit of fabric peeking out from behind the trash can that was tucked under the counter.

Addie's breath caught.

She recognized that pattern. It was the same fabric her aunt's purse was made of. Kate had bought the bag during Addie's last visit when they'd gone to the local arts and crafts fair. It looked like the purse had been shoved behind the trash can.

She narrowed her eyes. "Where were you between eleven and midnight last night?"

Zelda waved a hand. "I don't know. Asleep in my bed."

The front door rattled, and they both turned as two women in sun hats entered the store laughing over something.

Addie's heart jumped. Now was her chance!

She darted past Zelda and snatched the purse from under the counter. Then she hurried toward Chelsea.

"Go, go, let's get out of here," Addie hissed and sped up, aiming for the door with Chelsea on her heels.

"Hey!" Zelda shouted behind them. "What's that you have? Come back here! Thief!"

Addie nearly crashed into a tall, bookish-looking man in a cardigan as she sped out of the shop. Outside, she turned right and skidded to a stop at the entrance to Wild Rose, fumbling with the key.

Chelsea was right on her heels. Lucky ran up behind them, letting out a little excited bark.

Jamming the key in the lock, Addie turned it, threw the door open, and then held it for Chelsea and Lucky. Once everyone was inside, Addie slammed the door closed and turned the deadbolt.

Then she backed away, watching through the glass as her heart hammered.

"What was that all about?" Chelsea asked, slightly out of breath.

Addie held up the bag. "This is Kate's purse. It was jammed behind the trash can under the register."

Chelsea gasped. "Is her phone in there?"

Still watching the door and expecting Zelda to run up at any moment, Addie stuck her hand into the bag. A small stack of papers spilled to the floor.

Finally looking away from the door, Addie knelt to gather up the paperwork.

Chelsea came to help her. "What is this?" she asked, frowning.

At first glance, it appeared to be some sort of real estate paperwork.

"This can't be right," Addie said. She shuffled through the papers. "It looks like this is for the sale of Wild Rose's space to . . . Zelda Larson?"

"Did Kate ever say anything about closing up shop?"

"No," Addie said. "If anything, it was the opposite. She'd talked about creating a little consultation room in the back. And she added those tables and chairs. I don't for a second believe she wanted to sell."

"Maybe she decided to move to a different location," Chelsea suggested. "Maybe Zelda offered her enough money that Kate couldn't turn it down. She might get into a bigger space or move somewhere closer to the heart of downtown."

Addie shook her head. "My aunt loves it here."

She dug around in the bag some more and came up with a phone. She and Chelsea exchanged a look.

"I think I saw a charger behind the counter when we were cleaning up last night," Chelsea said.

Addie went and plugged in Kate's phone, breaking out into a cold sweat as she waited for it to power up. She touched the screen, and a number pad appeared.

"Do you know her code?" Chelsea asked.

"Yeah. I saw her tap it in dozens of times. She never tried to be secretive about it. She's always been so . . . trusting." Addie swallowed hard, as she couldn't help thinking that maybe Kate's trustful ways had ultimately gotten her in trouble.

Addie entered the passcode, and the phone unlocked. With shaking fingers, she navigated to texts. Not seeing anything out of the ordinary, she tapped the button to see the list of voicemails. There were several from her, which she skipped over. Then there were three from Zelda. Addie tapped the oldest of the three and put it on speakerphone.

"I've given you a week to think about it," came Zelda's voice through the speaker. "You'd be stupid not to take the deal. Besides which, you can run your business from anywhere. I can't move so easily, not with all my inventory, and you know I need more space. Just sign it, Kate. It's a good offer."

The other two messages were similar, but with Zelda growing more agitated as she insisted Kate take the deal. By the end of the most recent one, Zelda was shouting, and she even cursed before hanging up.

"Zelda's last message was left yesterday evening," Addie said.

She and Chelsea stared at each other for a long moment.

"Maybe we should contact the authorities," Chelsea said.

There was a sudden loud bang on the window, and they both jumped. Zelda stood there, red-faced.

"If you don't return what you stole, I'm going to call the police!" she shouted and gave the window a pound of her fist for emphasis.

Addie exchanged a confused look with Chelsea. "The police? Why would she want to call the police? She's the one who was hiding my aunt's purse!"

Walking forward with the bag in her hand, Addie faced Zelda through the glass door. "You had Kate's purse hidden under your counter," she said, lifting the bag. "If anyone should be calling the police, it's me."

Zelda's eyes widened, and a look of confusion laced with fear replaced her anger. She backed up, turned, and hurried away in the direction of the antique store.

Addie turned around to speak to Chelsea. "What is going on with that woman? Is she acting suspiciously, or am I imagining things?"

Chelsea's brow furrowed. "No, that was bizarre. Now we know she was trying to coerce Kate into selling her space, and that's motive. I heard her answer when you asked where she was last night, and it wasn't very convincing. I think we need to get the police involved."

"You're probably right. First, I'm going to call Bennett," Addie said, remembering what he'd told her about not trusting the police to be helpful in Kate's case.

The P.I. picked up after the first ring, and she quickly described what had taken place with Zelda.

"You're at Wild Rose?" he asked.

"Yes."

"Okay, don't move and don't call the police yet. I'll be there in five."

Addie hung up and watched through the window anxiously until she saw Bennett across the street. She waited until he was right at the door before unlocking it.

He was slightly out of breath when she let him in. She quickly introduced him to Chelsea.

"Do you think Zelda's the one who attacked Kate?" Addie asked.

Bennett was giving the real estate papers a quick look. He set them on the counter.

"It's hard to say for sure, but it doesn't look good for her," he said. "You say she was acting erratically?"

"Very," Addie said. She turned to her friend. "I mean, you saw it, too. She was the definition of erratic. And suspicious, if you ask me."

"I think there could be something else going on with Zelda," Chelsea said quietly.

"You don't think she did it?" Addie asked with a frown.

With an agitated flip of her blond hair over her shoulder, Chelsea opened her mouth and then closed it. "I . . . I'm not sure what I think. There's definitely something going on with Zelda, but there could be another explanation."

"But look at the facts." Addie spread her hands. "Zelda is angry. Mad enough to curse Kate out and more or less threaten her. Zelda was extremely skittish when I questioned her. And she was obviously trying to hide the purse. You can't deny that's pretty damning."

"It is, I just—I don't know. You're probably right," Chelsea said, still sounding unsure.

"Do you think we should call the police?" Addie asked Bennett.

He did that grimace thing again, the one that brought out his dimple. "You probably should. They can take Zelda's prints and see if they're a match for any of the ones they pulled from the scene."

This time when Addie called the police station and asked to be transferred, Julia McCann actually answered.

Addie described finding her aunt's purse at Zelda's A to Z Antiques and how Zelda had become irate with Kate.

"I'm going to need you to come to the station so I can take down your statement," Detective McCann said in her usual business-like tone.

"You need me to come in? Uh, okay. I guess can be there in a few minutes," Addie said.

But she couldn't help feeling deflated at the response. She'd expected the detective and the crime scene guy to race out to question Zelda and take her fingerprints.

Suddenly, Addie felt a little nervous. But that was silly. She hadn't done anything wrong.

"I have to go to the station," Addie told Chelsea and Bennett.

"We'll go with you," Chelsea said without hesitation. She glanced at the P.I. "Right?"

"Sure," he said. "But I'll take my own car and wait outside, if you don't mind. McCann and I haven't always seen eye to eye, and I don't want to bias her further by revealing my association with you."

Addie turned to Lucky, who'd been lying on the floor with his head on his paws. "I think you'll have to stay here, buddy."

He gave one thump of his tail, seeming okay with that suggestion. Addie went and got the water bowl from upstairs, topped it off, and left it near Lucky.

She slung her own small cross-body purse across her shoulder, grabbed Kate's slouchy bag with the phone and paperwork returned to it, and clutched the shop key in her hand.

"I'll go out first and wait while you get in your car," Bennett offered.

"Thank you," Addie said, relieved someone would be standing watch while she left the store and got into her Ford Escape. "I'm parked right out front."

With a slightly trembling hand, she locked up and then hurried over to her car. Chelsea slid into the passenger seat, and Addie hit the power locks and gave Bennett a little wave.

As she pulled away, she glanced in her rearview. The door to the antique store opened, and Zelda stood there, watching Addie leave.

A chill spilled down Addie's spine.

Had Zelda really attacked Aunt Kate?

Chapter Ten

ADDIE WENT INTO THE POLICE station alone. Detective McCann met her at the front desk and took her down a hallway to a room that looked more like a small corporate conference room than the interrogation rooms on TV.

Sitting across the table, the detective pulled out her little notebook.

"Why were you in the antique store?" she asked.

Addie opened her mouth, but surprise kept her from answering right away. Why did that question make it seem like she was the one being interrogated? She hesitated, knowing the longer she delayed her response, the worse it would make her look. But she couldn't rat out Bennett and the fact that he'd tracked Kate's phone to Zelda's.

"Yesterday I spoke to Zelda, and she seemed agitated when I brought up my aunt," Addie said. "I wanted to know why, because they've always been friends."

All true. Just not the whole truth.

"Could you repeat the conversation to the best of your memory?" Detective McCann asked.

Addie talked for a few minutes, trying to recall the exchange the best she could.

"And you say you saw the purse under the checkout counter."

"Yes," Addie said. "I recognized it because I was with my aunt when she bought it."

The detective gave her a piercing look. "You thought it was a good idea to snatch evidence and run away with it." It was phrased more as a critical statement than a question.

"I wasn't thinking in terms of preserving the crime scene," Addie said, feeling her cheeks heat.

"No kidding," McCann muttered under her breath. She tossed her notebook and pen on the table, leaned back, and folded her arms. "Here's the thing. Your amateur sleuthing really screwed things up. Now we only have your word on where Kate James's purse was found. If Ms. Larson denies it, it's your word against hers."

"Well, maybe she'll tell the truth," Addie said. "Plus, there's the voicemail. Zelda threatened Kate. She's obviously still pretty worked up. Aren't you even going to talk to her?"

"We'll ask her some questions, yes."

"What about getting her fingerprints?" Addie pressed.

The detective's expression clouded, her cheeks reddening to match her hair. Oops. Seemed like Addie had crossed some invisible line.

"You are not leading this investigation. You need to leave this to the authorities. To me," McCann said sternly. "If you keep interfering, you could ruin our chances at finding the culprit. What you did today was a serious mistake. It's against the law to interfere with a police investigation, did you know that?"

Addie shifted uncomfortably. "I wasn't trying to hinder you, though. I just really want to find out who hurt my aunt because I think that person will know where she is now."

"That's not your job." The detective stood. "If you really want to help your aunt, don't interfere. I'll let you know if there's anything I can report back to you. Do you remember the way out?"

Nodding and feeling like a kid who just got grounded, Addie slinked from the room and out of the station.

Back in the car with Chelsea, Addie covered her face with her hands and moaned. "That was pretty much awful," she said, looking up at her friend.

Bennett had come over to the car, so she rolled down the window and told him and Chelsea what'd happened with McCann.

The P.I. looked toward the station's entrance, his expression darkening. "I should go in there and talk to Julia."

"No, that's okay," Addie said quickly. "I've already ticked her off enough. I appreciate the offer, but I don't want to make her angrier."

He still looked like he wanted to give the detective a piece of his mind, which wasn't a good idea but gave Addie a little zing of pleasure. It was always good to have allies.

"It's about dinner time," Bennett said. "Why don't I pick up some food and we can regroup back at Wild Rose?"

Addie perked up. "That's awfully nice of you."

"Javier's Mexican okay?"

"Okay by me," Addie said, her stomach rumbling in approval. "I've been a little bit in love with Javier's chicken mole tacos since I was a teenager."

Bennett grinned. "Got it. How about you?" he asked Chelsea.

"A taco salad would be great," she said.

Addie unzipped her purse. "Here, let me give you some cash for ours."

He held up his hand. "No need. Your aunt's been good to me. The least I can do is buy her niece dinner."

"Thank you, Bennett," Addie said and was rewarded with a smile and the dimple.

"Meet you at Wild Rose." He crisply thumped the roof of the car with his palm twice and then turned to go.

Addie watched him for a moment. "Do you think he and Kate had some kind of fling?"

"No," Chelsea pronounced firmly and with no hesitation.

"That sounded awfully confident." Addie turned to her friend, who was still watching the P.I., and arched a brow. "Is this an aura thing?"

Chelsea nodded and then her gaze sharpened on Addie. "He's not interested in Kate. He's . . . interested in someone else."

"Oh. That's nice," Addie said absently, her mind already jumping to other things. "Mind if we stop at the market and pick up some dog food for Lucky? I should probably grab some things to have at the apartment, too."

At the grocery store, Addie filled her basket with a few groceries, a small bag of dog chow, and a leash, and she tried not to think about the fact that she no longer had a paycheck. Her savings would carry her for a little while, but at some point, she'd have to figure out her job situation.

Back at Wild Rose, Addie went upstairs to feed Lucky and put away the groceries in the kitchenette while Chelsea watched for Bennett through the locked front door.

Addie heard Bennett come in and then soft voices as he chatted with Chelsea. Actually, it almost sounded as if they were whispering. That seemed odd, seeing as how they'd only just met.

Partway down the stairs, Addie hesitated as she caught a snippet of the conversation below.

". . . long have you known about your ability?" Chelsea asked.

"Since I was a teenager," Bennett replied.

Whatever Chelsea said next was too muffled to make out.

Lucky bounded down the stairs past Addie, bringing the exchange to a halt. Addie descended slowly, pondering what Chelsea might have meant by "ability."

But then the delicious aroma of Mexican food pushed those thoughts away.

The three of them crowded around one of the café tables and dug into dinner. Bennett revealed he'd previously lived in Washington state, where he'd been a high school teacher for a short time. He spoke of the experience with a happy, yet wistful look in his eye.

"Why don't you teach anymore?" Addie asked.

"I'd like to. Maybe someday," he said, looking down at his enchiladas.

It seemed like a sensitive topic, so she didn't press him on it.

"Did you know Chelsea owns a boutique here in town?" Addie asked, to change the subject. "She has an incredible eye for fashion."

"Do you carry men's clothes?" Bennett asked. He gestured at his jeans and short-sleeved gray striped button down. "I could probably use some help in that department, as you can see."

"I don't carry menswear," Chelsea said. "But you don't give yourself enough credit. I saw the label on your pants. You're at least a little bit fashion-conscious to choose such an on-trend brand."

He gave a small laugh.

"Actually, what I really want to do is create my own line of clothing," Chelsea said.

"You do?" Addie asked. "You never mentioned that."

"I started taking sewing lessons a couple of years ago, and I've made a few pieces. Nothing I want to reveal publicly, though. I'm not good enough yet to make the actual pieces match what's in my mind."

Chelsea's revelation was surprising, considering she'd done it in front of someone she'd only just met. She was normally more reserved than her warm and friendly demeanor indicated. Addie couldn't help wondering if Chelsea was the one Bennett was interested in. There seemed to be a certain ease between them, if not an obvious chemistry or attraction.

Bennett turned his gaze to Addie. "And what about you? What's your secret heart's desire?"

The sudden earnestness in his eyes made Addie's heart bump.

She hesitated, fiddling with the edge of the container that held her dinner. "Well, I always wanted to be a doctor. I ended up going into research instead."

"It's not too late to follow your dream," Bennett said.

"Maybe," Addie said. "But there's no way I can think about that until Aunt Kate is home safe."

"Of course," he said quietly and with sympathy swimming in his dark-brown eyes.

Addie just couldn't accept the possibility of anything other than a happy outcome with her aunt's case, regardless of how strange and sinister it was. All three of them went silent for a minute or two.

Once they'd finished eating and cleaned up, Bennett wandered over to the apothecary shelves, seemingly in no hurry to go.

He turned to Addie. "Kate formulated an herbal remedy for me and I'm getting a little low. Do you think I could get more? I'll pay for it, of course."

"Sure," Addie said. "Do you happen to know what was in it?"

He shook his head. "Not in the right proportions, though I think I remember the ingredients. She has a notebook where she keeps those details."

"Oh right." Addie went to the counter and frowned. "It was here yesterday." She bent to look in the shelves below the counter, shuffling through papers, stacks of paper bags, rolls of receipt paper, and other items. She straightened with her hands on her hips. "That's odd. I know it was here."

"Do you think the person who attacked Kate stole it?" Chelsea asked, coming to peer into the shelves, too.

Addie's frowned deepened. "I . . . I don't know. I guess the police might have moved it. I'll keep looking." She turned to Bennett. "But in the meantime, if you want to tell me what's in your remedy, I can try to replicate it."

He looked a little uncertain. "Okay, we can try. That'd probably be better than nothing."

As he listed the names of herbs, Addie pulled liquid tincture preparations and lined them up. Then she got a clean amber dropper bottle from the cabinet under the apothecary shelves.

"Not knowing the precise proportions, I'm just going to do equal parts of each, if that's okay," she said, examining the ingredients. She was familiar with all of them, from past years helping out in the shop, and together they were most likely a remedy for insomnia. "These are all fairly gentle herbs, so having a bit more of any of them than you're used to shouldn't cause any problems."

"Okay, let's give it a shot," he said with a small shrug of one shoulder.

After mixing the tinctures and labeling the bottle, she handed it to Bennett. He reached back for his wallet, but she held up a hand.

"No way," she said. "If you were charging me your P.I. rate for what you did to find Kate's phone, I'd owe you way more than this. Plus, you already bought me dinner."

"Much appreciated," he said with a smile and nod.

He left not long after, and when Chelsea began yawning, Addie shooed her friend home as well.

"Are you sure?" Chelsea asked. "I can stay again, if you want."

Addie shook her head. "I'll be okay. I've got Lucky to protect me."

He wagged and ran a circle around Addie's feet.

Once she was alone, Addie spent a few minutes searching for Kate's apothecary notebook but came up empty. She faced Lucky.

"Okay, now would be a great time for your superpowers," she said. "Where's Aunt Kate's notebook?"

Lucky sat and looked up at her, and he gave a little whine. But after several seconds it was clear he either didn't know where the notebook was or he couldn't really understand her the way he'd seemed to that morning.

She bent down to scratch behind his ear. "That's okay, you don't need to do any magic to earn your keep. You can stay here as long as you like."

His tail swished back and forth in a blur, and she grinned.

It wasn't very late, but she was thinking about turning in so she could get an early start in the morning. Just as she shut off the shop lights, there was a tap at the door that startled her so badly she let out a little muffled scream.

"You're clearly not a watchdog," she mumbled to Lucky as she went toward the door.

All she could see in the window was a silhouette, and it looked like that of a woman. But it definitely wasn't Zelda. Still, Addie crept cautiously forward until she was close enough to recognize the young woman who'd been peering in the shop window earlier. It was Georgia, the girlfriend of Lance, who owned Ripped across the street.

Still uncertain, Addie gave a little wave. "Hi," she said loudly through the glass. "Can I help you?"

"Could I come in?" the young woman asked.

Addie hesitated. But Georgia looked so forlorn, and definitely not dangerous, so Addie slid the deadbolt back and opened the door.

With a furtive look over her shoulder, Georgia slipped inside.

"Did you need something from the shop?" Addie asked, locking the door just in case Zelda decided to show up.

"Yeah," Georgia said. She was dressed in yoga clothes and clutched the strap of her bag tightly over her shoulder.

"Oh, did you just come from a yoga class?" Addie asked, thinking she'd ask for a recommendation. It'd be nice to restart her yoga practice.

"No, martial arts," Georgia said in a clipped tone. "I'm trying to learn how to protect myself."

"Oh, that's cool. Well, my aunt, who's the owner, isn't here, but I can try to help you," Addie offered.

"I need your help," Georgia said. "But you can't tell anyone about this."

Addie tilted her head, unease stirring in her stomach. "Okay?"

"I'm pregnant." Addie was about to congratulate her when Georgia continued, "But I can't have this child."

Chapter Eleven

ADDIE'S LIPS PARTED, AND SHE blinked a couple of times.

"So, you want something to . . ." She trailed off.

"Yes," Georgia said. "Something to end it."

The lights were out in the shop and the sun had set. It wasn't full dark yet, but Georgia's face was cast in shadow. Even without seeing her expression, Addie could sense the woman's fear.

"But—Georgia, that's your name, right?" Addie asked.

"Yes. Look, I know Kate has a formula for this."

"How do you know that?"

"Because I was here the day before yesterday and asked her about it."

"So why didn't she give it to you?" Addie asked.

"She didn't want to," Georgia said impatiently. "She thought I'd change my mind. But I haven't. Could you just give it to me?"

"I'm sorry, but I don't know that particular formula," Addie said. "And even if I did, I wouldn't be comfortable—"

Georgia's hand darted out to clutch Addie's arm, cutting her off, and her heart lurched in alarm. "I know you've worked with your aunt. She talked about you. She said she trained you. I know you know what I need. Please, can you just help me? I need—I need it to look like the pregnancy ended naturally."

Addie shook her head and pulled her arm back. Lucky, who was behind her, let out a low growl.

"Can't you see I'm begging you?" Georgia said, her voice rising in pitch.

With a sinking stomach, Addie was beginning to realize opening the door had been a huge mistake.

"I'm sure there's a clinic that can help you, if you really need it," she said, going for a soothing tone.

"No, I told you," Georgia said. "It has to look like it ended naturally." She peered over her shoulder, and something she saw made her go rigid. She swore under her breath.

Addie squinted through the window. She saw Lance moving around in Ripped. And next door, Renaldo was locking up Hair Affair.

Visibly shaking, Georgia turned to her again. "I need it *now*, don't you understand?" Tears had started leaking down her cheeks.

"I'm so sorry, but I can't help you," Addie said.

Georgia covered her eyes with one hand, beginning to sob in earnest. But when her hand fell away, her posture and tone changed.

"This is supposed to be a place where people can come for remedies. For help," Georgia said forcefully, her voice going hoarse as it rose in volume. "But I guess without Kate here, that's no longer the case, is it?" She flung her arm out, seeming to indicate something in the shop.

Turning to see what Georgia was pointing at, Addie's hands flew to her lips when she realized the woman appeared to be gesturing at the very spot where Kate had collapsed.

Then Georgia whirled around, jerked the deadbolt back, and fled from the store.

Addie clenched her hand into a fist and pressed it into her stomach. Her breath was coming too fast. She locked the door and then sank to the floor.

Had Georgia really just pointed at the place where Addie had discovered her aunt? No, it couldn't be. Addie had just grown so suspicious of everyone her imagination was acting up.

From where she sat on the floor, Addie watched Georgia hurry across the street. Renaldo looked up, startled, as he was walking away from the salon. He and Georgia exchanged a few words, and then he walked away with his head down while she stood for a moment, out of the line of sight from within Ripped, and took some deep breaths. She swiped under her eyes, plastered on a smile, and went inside the supplement shop.

Addie didn't have a great view into Ripped because the signs and posters in the doors and windows obscured things somewhat, but it appeared Georgia and Lance were having an unhappy exchange inside. She kept watching until the couple disappeared into the back of the store.

Pulling out her phone, she slowly rose and retreated from the door after one last glance at the lock to make sure it was secured.

"C'mon, Lucky," she said weakly, and the dog followed her upstairs.

Addie curled up in a corner on the daybed, still shaken by what had just happened, and called Bennett. It wasn't that she didn't trust Chelsea, but Addie wanted some guidance from a professional about what to do next. Letting out a relieved breath when he answered, she described her encounter with Georgia.

"Do you think she could have attacked Kate?" Addie asked.

"She certainly sounds desperate," he said. His voice, deep and soothing, relaxed her a bit. "I think it's worth checking her alibi."

Addie chewed on the end of her thumb. "I'm not sure she'd be receptive if I tried to question her. She was pretty upset with me."

"I could do it."

"Yeah, but wouldn't that be weird? Some guy she doesn't know asking her what she was doing two nights ago around midnight?"

He let out a sigh. "You're probably right. I don't want you to put yourself in an uncomfortable situation, though."

"I appreciate that, but I think I need to do it. It's worth it, if it eliminates a suspect. Or adds one to the list. Whatever gets me one step closer to the person who knows where Kate is."

"I don't like it, but I think you're right. How about if I do some electronic investigation on her?" Bennett asked. "Background and social media checks, that sort of thing?"

"That would be great," Addie said. "I should probably let you go. I've already taken up a ton of your time today."

"No worries at all, Addie," he said. "Good night."

"Talk to you soon. Bye."

Addie got ready for bed and then burrowed under the blankets with Lucky at her feet and the TV on with the volume low. She thought she'd be wide awake for hours, but the day had taken its toll and she fell asleep within a few minutes.

─◦⟋⟍◦─

THE NEXT MORNING AS ADDIE stood in her sweats making coffee, there was a knock at the door downstairs. She checked the time. Only seven thirty. Way too early for customers.

Ugh. She wasn't in any sort of state for talking to the public. Couldn't they see the closed sign?

She went partway down and peered at the front door. Her breath stilled when she recognized Georgia. Tempted to backtrack and pretend she hadn't heard, Addie started to turn around. But Georgia spotted her and waved furiously. Still, Addie hesitated.

She didn't *have* to answer the door. Especially after Georgia's meltdown the previous night.

But then she held up something, pressing it against the glass.

Was that . . .?

Addie went down the stairs, slowly approaching the front, as her heart thudded. When she was still ten feet from the door, she inhaled a sharp breath.

Georgia had Aunt Kate's apothecary notebook.

Striding forward, Addie's insides swirled with conflicting emotions. Had Georgia stolen the notebook? Had she attacked Kate and taken it and now had the gall to show up with it? Why would she bring it back at all?

Addie stood at the door and crossed her arms. "How did you get that?" she demanded though the glass.

"I found it last night after I was here," Georgia said. "I wanted to come back and apologize anyway. I'm so sorry about the way I acted. You didn't deserve that, and I'm embarrassed. You don't have to let me in. I just wanted you to have this."

She started to bend down to leave the notebook outside the door.

"Don't go yet," Addie said, and Georgia straightened. "Where did you find it?"

Georgia's eyes slanted off to the side. "Uh, just on the ground."

"But where exactly?"

"In the alley behind the store." Georgia pointed over her shoulder with her thumb.

"Outside the back exit of Ripped?" Addie asked.

"Yeah. Anyway, I'm really sorry, and I just wanted to give you this. But I've gotta go." Georgia left the notebook propped against the door and started to move away.

"Wait," Addie hollered through the glass. "I need to ask you something."

Georgia looked nervous but reluctantly retraced her steps.

"Where were you two nights ago between eleven and midnight?" Addie asked.

"At the Grinning Catfish Brewery for their late-night Thirsty Thursday happy hour," Georgia said.

The brewery was only half a block away.

"What time did you get there, and what time did you leave?"

"Uh, I don't know, we got there maybe around ten. We left close to one."

"We being you and Lance?" Addie asked.

She nodded. "I really have to go." Head down, she walked swiftly off to the right.

Addie watched for a second to verify Georgia wasn't going to lurk nearby and then looked the other way to make sure Zelda wasn't poised to try to ambush Wild Rose. Satisfied the coast was clear, Addie unlocked the door, stuck her arm out, grabbed the notebook, and secured the bolt again.

A few steps away from the front, she froze. Oh, shoot. Maybe she should have picked up the notebook with a tissue like they did on TV. Had she just contaminated another piece of evidence? McCann would probably throw Addie in jail for obstruction of justice. Or whatever it was the detective had threatened.

Going behind the counter, she pulled up the stool she'd seen her aunt perch on so many times over the years as she chatted with customers or went through paperwork.

Addie opened the spiral-bound pad, flipping through pages that were dated years back. It was a hefty notebook, maybe an inch and a half thick. As expected, the entries listed custom herbal formulas that Kate had created for her clients. But there were also odd symbols, some of which looked vaguely familiar.

A swirling sensation began to take root in Addie's chest, quickly turning into an intense tingle that spread outward. With each turn of a page, the feeling intensified. After a few minutes, she stopped, closed her eyes, and pinched the bridge of her nose, hoping it would pass.

Maybe her blood sugar was low. Or the stress was getting to her. Maybe she was on the verge of a heart attack and this was the end.

"Get a grip," she muttered to herself.

With a sharp inhale meant to clear her head, she went back to looking through the notebook. But the sensation returned tenfold. She pulled her hand away as her heart punched her ribs in alarm—and in recognition.

She'd felt this before. When she'd looked into the teacup and the detailed little images had danced before her eyes, it had been almost the same unsettling physical experience.

What was happening?

Placing her hands on either side of the notebook, she looked down at it reluctantly, half afraid she was going to hallucinate again. But her vision remained unblurred, and the tingling began to subside.

That was a relief. She should put the notebook away. It was Kate's private record, and Addie shouldn't be reading it anyway.

And yet . . .

She bit her lower lip. She was a scientist. The least she could do was confirm cause and effect, even if she didn't understand the phenomenon.

Scooping up the notebook, she gripped it in both hands. The tingling surged from her chest outward, pins and needles dancing down every nerve. She sucked in a breath and firmed her grip, expecting the whispering voice to come as it had when she'd peered at the tea leaves.

But it didn't. After a minute or so, the tingling reached its peak and stayed there. It was uncomfortable, but not unbearable.

Addie dropped the notebook, waited a minute, and repeated the experiment.

Same result.

"Huh." She sat back, tapping her chin with her index finger.

Scientific curiosity had kicked in, overriding how disconcerting the experience was. Her gaze slid to the jars of loose tea. She hopped up and went back to the utility sink, retrieving the cup and saucer with the little dolphins on them that still sat on the drying rack.

Back in the storefront, she heated water and made tea the way she had before, dropping the herbs straight into the cup. Seeking to repeat the previous experience as exactly as possible, she carried the steaming cup, balanced on its saucer, to the table where she'd sat previously.

Her pulse skipped along as she drank the tea, thinking of how much she wished Aunt Kate were there and wondering what had happened to her.

When there was only a bit of liquid left, she overturned the cup on the saucer and then righted it.

Furious tingling gripped her heart, exploding like fireworks through her blood vessels.

It all came rushing back. The blurring. The very same intricate little images.

A flower inside a bottle.

The head of a smiling woman with the shape of a brain floating above her.

A capital L underlined by a slim knife.

Two stick figures with a lightning bolt separating them.

And the whispers.

This time, she listened.

"Not dead, but not alive. Not dead, but not alive. Not dead, but not alive."

The whispers repeated the same phrase over and over for a minute or two, and then began to fade.

Addie pushed the saucer away and took a moment to center herself.

"Not dead, but not alive," she said quietly.

The foremost worry in her mind had been whether or not her aunt had survived the attack. Kate's death was the thing she was most afraid of. The voices seemed to be addressing that central question, but the answer didn't make much sense. Maybe Kate was in a coma?

Addie pulled out her phone and called the two hospitals in the area. It only took a few minutes to confirm that there were no unidentified, unconscious women at either of them.

Recalling the little pictures in the leaves—which had been exactly the same as before—Addie closed her eyes, focusing on the memory of them.

She still wasn't sure what the symbols meant, but she knew one thing. She needed to see what was west of Pine Avenue. That was where Bennett had seen Aunt Kate heading the day she'd been attacked. There was some sort of hidden community out there. Maybe someone from that part of town had followed Kate home and attacked her. No one wanted to tell Addie what was going on in west Stargaze.

So, she'd just have to see for herself.

With renewed energy, she ran up the stairs to change. Lucky jumped off the daybed and yipped excitedly.

"I'm going to have a little adventure," she said to him. "Want to come?"

He let out a bark and wagged his tail.

Five minutes later, she had her car keys in one hand and the end of Lucky's new leash in the other. She went out into the morning sun, locked Wild Rose, put Lucky in the back seat, and hopped behind the wheel.

It was time to find some answers.

Chapter Twelve

ADDIE EASED AWAY FROM THE curb and then headed north on Pine Avenue, intending to take a left on Main Street. But when she got to the intersection of Pine and Main, the neon Open sign in Hair Affair's window flipped on. Spotting Renaldo inside, on a whim she made the turn and then pulled over.

Leaving the car parked in the shade and Lucky inside with the windows down, she hurried across the street toward the salon. Inside, Renaldo was alone restocking hair products on the glass shelving in the waiting area.

He looked up. "Hi, we don't do walk-ins, but would you like an appointment?"

"Uh, not today," Addie said. "I wanted to introduce myself. I'm Addie James."

"Renaldo Hernandez. You must be related to Kate."

She nodded. "I'm her niece."

"Sure, I remember you from when you've come to town before. I heard she'd had some kind of trouble," he said.

"Yeah," Addie replied. "She's missing, actually."

His brows pulled together. "Oh no, I'm so sorry."

"Thank you. I'm going to check out some places where she might have been recently," Addie said. "But while I'm here, I was wondering what Georgia said to you last night. I'd just spoken to her, and she was pretty upset. I wanted to see if she was okay."

He ran a hand over his fashionably spiked hair. "Yeah, she did seem distraught, but I didn't notice that right away. When I saw her, I asked her if she was going to Grinning Catfish on Saturday for their trivia night. I'd seen her there on Thursday."

"You were there with her on Thursday?"

"Not with her, but I stopped in for a quick drink before coming back here to do some work, and we talked for a couple of minutes."

"It must have been late when you got back here to the salon," Addie said. "Do you remember what time you left?"

His eyes tightened, and she didn't blame him. Her questions probably seemed a little odd.

"Yeah, after midnight," he said slowly. He touched the back of his neck and then folded his arms, his gaze swinging off to the side.

Addie's breath caught. Could he have witnessed something?

"Did you happen to see anyone around Wild Rose while you were here working that night?"

"I don't think so. I was in the back most of the time." His shoulders had inched up, his whole body tensed.

"Are you sure?" Addie pressed.

"Pretty sure."

"Did anyone happen to be with you?"

"I was alone the whole time," he said, his words rushed.

The way his eyes skipped past her, refusing to meet her gaze, gave her the impression he wasn't being completely truthful.

"Oh, here's my appointment," he said, looking relieved as the door opened and a blond woman with an inch of dark roots walked in. "Good to meet you, Addie."

She wanted to keep questioning but couldn't in front of his client. Plus, she had a feeling she'd just get the same answers. And she was equally sure that somewhere in the conversation Renaldo had been lying.

As she walked out, she glanced at someone standing across the street on the corner looking her way. It was the tall man who looked like a professor who she'd nearly run into the previous day in her rush to get out of Zelda's. He was smiling warmly and waving, and she nearly waved back before she realized he wasn't looking at her. She peered into the salon to see Renaldo with a broad grin on his face. He winked at the man across the street and flipped him a little wave.

When the bookish man realized Addie was watching, his smile fell abruptly, he ducked his head, and he turned and hurried into the corner shop, a bookstore called Enchanted Pages.

Hmm. Interesting.

But she couldn't ponder it further because she needed to get on with her mission to explore the west part of Stargaze.

She got back in her car, which she'd parked next to a yoga and Pilates studio, and continued west past the law office and the eerie street she'd walked down to get to Bennett's office.

The warehouse he'd mentioned took up the next block. She also passed rows and rows of self-storage units, as well as the trucking company.

After several blocks, the area shifted from industrial to residential. But it wasn't a pretty neighborhood like many in Stargaze. There were run-down apartment buildings with tired landscaping and cracked sidewalks. Despite all the housing, there were very few people out and about.

Addie started to think maybe there weren't many residents in these apartments, but most of the balconies had lawn chairs, bicycles, barbecues, potted plants, and other items that were evidence of the occupants.

She pulled over, intending to look up the address of the soup kitchen where Kate volunteered, but her phone rang before she could do the search. It was Bennett.

"Just wanted to let you know that I've confirmed Georgia's story," he said with no preamble.

"She was at Thirsty Thursday from ten until one in the morning?"

"Well, she was there, but I can't say for sure that she stayed there the whole time," he said. "It's not the most solid alibi in the world, especially considering how close Grinning Catfish Brewery is to Wild Rose Teas and Apothecary."

"Actually, she stopped by this morning," Addie said. She went on to describe how Georgia had apologized and returned Kate's notebook that had supposedly been discarded in the alley. "Georgia acted so strangely last night, but why would she bring the notebook back if she was the one who attacked Kate? If Georgia was the attacker, it'd be pretty stupid of her to tie herself to Wild Rose and that night."

Bennett let out a breath. "You know, I'm inclined to agree with you. It'd be good if we could find someone who could confirm that she didn't leave Grinning Catfish during the hour in question, but my gut tells me she's not the culprit."

"And what's your gut's track record?" Addie asked in a serious tone.

He laughed, a deep warm sound that made her grin. "It's pretty darn good, if I do say so myself."

"Something else happened this morning that I should probably mention," she said and then described her exchange with Renaldo in the salon. "I have this funny feeling he's hiding something."

"How's *your* gut's track record?" Bennett asked teasingly.

"If I'm being honest, I'm not great at listening to my instincts," she said. "I tend to rely more on logic. But human beings aren't the most rationally behaving creatures, so where people are concerned, that approach often comes back to bite me in the butt."

"Well, both approaches have their place. And in any case, file Renaldo away and we can circle back to him if needed."

"Sounds good," she said.

"Is that a car engine? Are you headed out somewhere?" he asked.

"Uh, yeah, just need to pick up a few things," Addie said.

The white lie didn't feel great when Bennett had been so helpful, but he'd been adamant about Addie steering clear of the secret community in west Stargaze.

"I think it'd be wise to revisit Lisette as a suspect," he said. "Maybe Enzo, too. Their alibis were both mushy, and I'd like to firm them up if possible."

"Okay, I can help out with that after I get back," Addie said. "I'll give you a call."

"Looking forward to it," Bennett said.

A fresh wave of gratitude swept through her. He seemed almost as invested in Kate's case as Addie was, and she was still counting her lucky stars that he'd sought her out. It didn't hurt that he was attractive and good-hearted, too.

"Thanks, me too," she said.

She found the address of the soup kitchen, Bowl of Plenty, and headed in that direction. When she arrived, she parked half a block away and killed the engine. Then she watched as people trickled in. A check of her phone indicated it was early for lunch, but the kitchen's website said it opened at ten o'clock every day and it was a quarter past.

While she was observing, an older gold Mercedes in pristine condition pulled into Bowl of Plenty's lot. Addie's eyes popped wide when a familiar woman got out. It was Betty.

What in the world was Betty doing there? Addie was pretty sure the mystic wasn't a volunteer. And besides, the emporium should have been open at that time of day. Why had Betty closed her store to come here?

The mystic was dressed in one of her signature shift dresses, this one sleeveless with yellow and blue stripes. She didn't go in the front entrance of the soup kitchen. Instead, she entered through a side door off the parking lot.

Addie got out, intending to see what Betty was doing, but Lucky started barking when Addie tried to walk away from the car.

"Okay, you can come," she said, going back. "But we have to be quiet. We're trying to keep a low profile."

She grabbed the end of his leash, and he hopped to the ground. Then they scurried across the street.

Addie headed toward the soup kitchen's side door, but Lucky pulled at the leash when they reached the Mercedes. She tugged gently, but he refused to move, sitting back on his haunches. Then he went over to the car and stood up on his hind legs, placing his front paws on the passenger door.

"You wanna go for a ride in the nice car?" she asked.

He poked his nose at the door.

She glanced through the passenger window and did a double take. There was a plastic shopping bag from a drug store on the front seat, and some of the items had spilled out. Addie's eyes narrowed at the light-blue bottle lying on its side. She knew that bottle. It was the shampoo in Aunt Kate's shower, the exact brand and scent she'd used for years. And was that a container of the natural salt and charcoal deodorant she used, too?

"What the . . ." Addie muttered under her breath.

"Hello there, dearie," called a voice behind her.

Addie stiffened, her heart lurching guiltily like a kid with her hand caught in the cookie jar. Turning, she found Betty hurrying—as much as a woman of her size could hurry—toward the car.

"Betty, what are you doing here?" Addie asked. She was a little embarrassed she'd been caught, but her need for answers overrode her discomfort. "And why do you have Kate's favorite toiletries in your car?"

The mystic's hands fluttered at her chest. "Oh, well, I wanted to see if I could fill in here for Kate."

"And the products?" Addie pointed at the window.

"Well, you know, Kate has recommended these things to me over the years, and I've started using them myself."

Addie tilted her head, scrutinizing Betty's expression. In Addie's visits to the emporium the past couple of days, the mystic hadn't smelled like either the shampoo or the deodorant, both of which had distinct scents that Addie associated with her aunt.

Betty was lying about the products and also possibly about volunteering. Addie was nearly certain of it.

"What's going on?" Addie asked. She pointed at the soup kitchen. "Is Kate in there?"

"No, dearie, of course not," Betty said gently.

Blasting out a breath, Addie ran a hand over her hair. "Betty, I don't think you're telling me the truth. And—and I think Kate is alive somewhere, but she might be hurt. Maybe in a coma. Or drugged. I don't know exactly, but I think she's in an incapacitated state. If you're taking supplies to her, you *have* to tell me. I'm her family. I have a right to know."

Betty's gaze sharpened. "Why do you think Kate is incapacitated somewhere?"

"I did another tea-leaf reading. I don't really believe that stuff, but there were voices like before. This time, I listened to them."

The mystic was leaning forward, her attention trained intently on Addie. "What did you hear?" she asked, her voice low.

"They said, 'Not dead, but not alive,'" Addie said. "I think they were talking about Aunt Kate."

The back of her neck and her chest had dampened with a cold sweat. She pressed her hands against her thighs to try to stop the slight trembling.

Betty nodded almost imperceptibly and drew back. "You need to go home, Addie," she said.

"I'm not going to go home. If she's out there, I need to find her. Especially if she's hurt or unconscious."

"You can't help her. Not right now."

Addie stared at the mystic and then swallowed hard. "Does that mean she's . . . alive?"

"Go back home," was all Betty would say. She went around to the driver side, got in, and started the engine.

"Wait," Addie said, knocking frantically on the passenger window. "You have to tell me what's going on! Do you know where she is?"

But Betty backed out of the parking spot and pulled away, accelerating down the street.

"Just tell me," Addie ground out through clenched teeth.

She ran toward her car, intending to follow Betty, but she already knew it was too late. The Mercedes was gone.

Standing at her Ford Escape with Lucky's leash in one hand and her keys in the other, Addie fought back tears.

Was Betty confirming what the voices said, that Kate wasn't dead? Why couldn't anyone just come out and say what was going on?

A vibration and jangle from her purse startled her. Juggling her keys, she pulled her phone out. It was Bennett calling.

"I did some poking around and discovered Georgia wasn't at Grinning Catfish Brewery the entire time on Thursday like she said." His words came in a rush. "Both of the brewery owners remember her leaving for about forty-five minutes around the time Kate was attacked. And I've got another witness who says he saw her looking in the window of Wild Rose at around eleven thirty."

Addie gasped. "What? Are you serious?"

"I've got her here in my office. She's finally admitted she left the brewery but refuses to say what she was doing while she was gone," he said. "I thought you might want to talk to her yourself before we call the police."

"I'll be there in five minutes," she said.

In a blur of movement, Addie lifted Lucky into the back and jumped in the front, started the engine, and roared away.

Her heart pounded the whole way to Bennett's office.

She parked in front, grabbed Lucky's leash, and ran inside and up the stairs.

When she arrived at the office, Bennett let her in. Georgia was sitting on one of the folding chairs, her eyes puffy and red and a miserable look on her face.

"I didn't hurt Kate, I swear," she said. "You have to believe me."

"Georgia, you lied about that night," Addie said. "You weren't at Thirsty Thursday the whole time like you said. So why should we believe you didn't attack my aunt?"

"Because I didn't," Georgia said, her voice pitching high with desperation.

"You think she could have overtaken Kate?" Bennett asked Addie.

"They're the same size and build, but Georgia told me something last night that would give her an edge over my aunt," Addie said. "She takes martial arts classes."

The P.I. pressed his lips together and nodded grimly.

Addie pulled out her phone. "I'm calling Detective McCann."

Chapter Thirteen

THE NEXT FIFTEEN MINUTES WHILE they waited for Detective McCann were, well, awkward. Addie was just glad Georgia didn't try to leave because what would they do if she did? It wasn't like Addie and Bennett had the right to physically stop her. But Georgia just sat in the chair, dejected.

Addie tried a few times to ask what Georgia had been doing when she left the brewery Thursday night, but she continued to refuse to answer.

"I know you're afraid," Addie said quietly. "But you're not going to get out of this. You're going to have to confess. I'd really like to know what happened to my aunt. And frankly, the police can deal with the attack and robbery. I just want to know where she is now."

Georgia shook her head. "I don't have any idea where she is. And I'm not the one who hurt her, so there's nothing to confess."

When Detective McCann finally arrived, she was accompanied by Officer Davis.

"You," the detective said to Bennett. "You're mixed up in this? I should have known."

Bennett, to his credit, held his tongue. He gave Addie a slight roll of his eyes when Detective McCann wasn't looking.

Officer Davis had given Addie a nod when he came in and then took up a post at the door, presumably to stop Georgia from bolting.

"Okay," Detective McCann said with a sigh. "What's going on here?"

Addie let Bennett explain what he'd discovered. Then she recounted how threatening Georgia had acted the previous night at Wild Rose but left out the part about Georgia wanting to end her pregnancy. And, of course, McCann picked up on the omission.

"What did Georgia need a remedy for?" the detective asked.

"You'll have to ask her," Addie said.

McCann faced Georgia. "Well?"

Georgia miserably stared at the floor. "I don't want to say."

"Fine. We'll skip that for the moment. But we need to know where you were the night Kate James was attacked."

"I didn't hurt her," Georgia said. "I can prove it."

"How?" Addie asked, and was rewarded with a sharp, irritated look from the detective.

"I'll ask the questions," McCann said and then turned back to Georgia. "Can someone corroborate your claim?"

Georgia nodded. "His name is Woodrow Chatterton."

Addie's brow furrowed. "Chatterton, like the name on the law office sign behind Hair Affair?"

"Woodrow is one of the lawyers in that firm," Bennett confirmed quietly when McCann ignored Addie's question.

"And what were you doing with Mr. Chatterton?" McCann asked.

"Talking to him." Georgia's cheeks reddened.

"Why?"

"I . . . Oh, hell," Georgia muttered. She straightened and cleared her throat. "I've been involved with Woodrow. Yes, that kind of involved. I'm pregnant with his child."

Addie's eyes popped wide.

"You were with him the entire time you were absent from Grinning Catfish?" McCann asked.

"Yes," Georgia said.

"That's a lie!" Addie jumped in. "Renaldo saw her look in the window of Wild Rose."

Georgia grasped her forehead. "Sorry, yes, I did do that. Right before I went to Woodrow's office. But that's all I did, just look in the window."

McCann heaved an exasperated sigh. "Okay. Here's what's going to happen. Officer Davis is going to find Woodrow Chatterton and question him. And in the meantime, Georgia's going to relinquish her phone and come with me to the station to wait, so we know she's not in communication with Woodrow."

"Am I under arrest?" Georgia asked, her eyes wide.

"No, but I'd like you to stay at the station until we can confirm your alibi," McCann said. "It would be in your best interest to cooperate, because if you don't it only makes you look suspicious."

Georgia nodded and stood.

McCann paused at the door at looked back at Addie. "I warned you already to stop interfering. I see you're trying to get around it by hiring your own investigator. But I've got news for you. This is your last warning. Next time you take matters into your own hands, I'll charge both of you with obstruction."

Georgia, Julia McCann, and Officer Davis departed, leaving Addie, Bennet, and Lucky alone.

Addie sank onto the chair where Georgia had been a moment ago. "Well, that was . . . disappointing." She shook her head. "It really seemed like Georgia was the one. Maybe she *did* do it. Maybe they won't be able to confirm her alibi."

"I don't think she's the culprit," Bennett said.

"Your gut again?"

He gave her a wry look and a nod. "And I've seen scenarios like this before, where someone's lying, but not about the thing you think. Most people aren't criminals, but most people *do* have things they don't want anyone to know. People lie to hide their secrets. Georgia obviously has some big ones."

Addie was quiet for a moment, absently reaching down to scratch the back of Lucky's neck.

"Her boyfriend, Lance, is probably going to find out about the affair," Addie said.

"I think Renaldo knew about it," Bennett said. "He only said he saw Georgia look in the window at Wild Rose, but I'm guessing he's probably seen her and Woodrow together."

"It makes sense. His salon is right in back of the law firm, basically right between there and Ripped. If Georgia was meeting Woodrow at his office, Renaldo easily could have seen or overheard something." She scrunched her mouth to one side as something nagged at the back of her mind. "If you're right about that, then I think that's more evidence that Renaldo is holding back."

"Could be he just doesn't want to get any more involved than he has to. Or maybe he's trying to keep from having to talk about someone else's infidelity. I wouldn't blame him. That's some messy business to get mixed up in."

"True," Addie agreed.

She couldn't seem to summon the energy to stand up, walk down the stairs, and get on with the day. Some small part of her was still hoping Georgia was the attacker and would be found out, so Addie could demand Georgia be pressed about where Kate was. But Addie suspected Bennett was right. And that meant the culprit, the one who probably knew her aunt's location, was still out there somewhere.

"Are you okay?" Bennett asked, coming to sit on the edge of his desk near Addie.

"I just want to find Aunt Kate, and now it feels like I'm no closer than before."

"Well, think of it this way," he said. "If Georgia's alibi checks out, we can eliminate her from the suspect pool. Even a negative result gives us information."

Addie brightened the tiniest bit. "That's what we used to say in the lab. Even a failed experiment is a result. All results give you information."

They traded small smiles, and she got to her feet.

"Thank you again for all of your help," she said. "I don't know how I can ever repay you."

He gave a modest half-shrug. "I'm happy to do it."

Addie packed Lucky into the car and then drove around the corner to Wild Rose, where she parked in the front.

Trudging inside, she locked the door behind her and went upstairs to make a sandwich. After she halfheartedly ate part of it, her phone rang.

"Hey, Chelsea," she answered.

"Hi. I'm so sorry I didn't call earlier. I nearly forgot to put in some orders today, so I had to catch up on that."

"Oh, that's okay," Addie said. "But you missed quite an eventful morning."

She spent the next few minutes catching Chelsea up on what had transpired with Georgia.

"How are you doing with it all, hon?" Chelsea asked.

"I got my hopes up there for a minute," Addie said. "But I'll get over it. If anything, I'm more determined than ever to figure out who attacked Kate. I can't give up hope the person will know where she is now."

"Sounds like you'll have to be careful if you wanna keep Julia McCann off your back," Chelsea said.

"Yeah, no kidding." Addie chewed the inside of her cheek for a minute. "You're welcome to come by when you get off work, if you want to."

"I'd love to. I'll text you before I leave."

"Okay, talk to you soon. Bye, Chelsea."

Addie sat staring off into space, thinking about the emotional rollercoaster she'd been on that morning. Her conversation with Betty outside Bowl of Plenty came back to the forefront of Addie's thoughts, and that reminded her of what she'd seen in the tea leaves.

Finding the photo of the soggy herbs in the teacup on her phone, she set it down, went and got a sheet of paper from Kate's printer downstairs, and sat at the little dining table in the living room.

Using the photo to help jog her memory, she started sketching the symbols she'd seen outlined in the teacup. Then she sat back and examined her drawings.

What could they mean?

If Betty was correct, they all had something to do with what'd happened to Kate because that was what Addie had been focused on when she'd sipped the tea.

She started with the smiling head with the floating brain because it seemed the strangest of the four images. Maybe the brain meant intelligence? Perhaps the smiling person was Addie, who was supposed to use her science smarts to help her aunt.

Addie moved on to the L with the knife underlining it. The knife had to mean violence. And if so, then the L could be the initial of the attacker. Lisette? She hadn't been completely ruled out as a suspect, and since it appeared Georgia would be cleared, Lisette was back in play.

Just as Addie was about to closely examine the two stick figures with a lightning bolt separating them, there was a loud knock on the door downstairs.

She went down, hoping it was Chelsea, but it wasn't.

Julia McCann stood there with a paper bag in her hand.

Addie groaned. Was she in trouble with the detective for something new?

She reluctantly went and unlocked the door.

"I hoped you'd be here," McCann said. "Can I come in?"

"Sure," Addie said without enthusiasm.

"I thought you'd want to know that we cleared Georgia. Woodrow Chatterton corroborated her claim, and his business partner Craig Bledsoe backed it up. Apparently, he was at the office late that night, too."

Addie nodded, not really surprised but still disappointed. "I appreciate the update, Detective."

McCann held up the paper bag. "I thought you might like this back. It's your aunt's purse."

Addie took the offered bag. "Does this mean Zelda Larson isn't a suspect anymore, either?"

"She claims she was at home asleep the night of the attack. Until we have something that tells us otherwise, we really can't pursue her as a suspect. There's not enough for an arrest."

Addie frowned. "She didn't seem entirely sure about her answer when I asked her where she was that night. And I would think hiding my missing aunt's purse would be more than a little damning."

"It doesn't make her look good, I'll grant you that," McCann said. "But it's not enough."

Addie disagreed, but pushing would only get her more lectures about keeping out of the way of the investigators.

"I appreciate you returning my aunt's things," Addie said. "But my biggest concern is finding Kate. She's out there somewhere, and the more time that passes, the more I'm afraid . . . I just really want to find her."

"We've had officers out questioning people to see if anyone might have seen her since the attack. We'll try to get the local news station to run something."

"Oh, that would be great," Addie said with genuine gratitude. "Please keep me in the loop of any developments."

"If there's anything we can report to you, we will," McCann said.

The detective left, but before Addie could lock up, Chelsea appeared in the window.

Addie held the door for her.

"Hey," Chelsea said. "I got done earlier than I thought. I texted you but figured I might as well just come over."

"Oh, sorry, my phone's upstairs, and I must have missed it," Addie said. She hefted the bag. "Detective McCann was just here returning Aunt Kate's purse."

"That was nice," Chelsea said.

"She also told me Georgia is officially cleared."

Chelsea's face fell. "Honey, I'm sorry."

Addie shrugged. "It wasn't really a surprise."

"Still, it's rough to go back to square one."

Addie's gaze unfocused for a moment as she thought about the visions in the tea leaves. Wasn't it worth pursuing those to the fullest extent possible if they could actually help?

Yes. At that point, Addie had to use everything at her disposal. Even the tea leaves, if necessary.

Addie took a deep breath. "Hey, Chelsea? I've got something to show you. It's upstairs."

Upstairs, Addie sat down at the table, and Chelsea slid into the seat across from her.

Addie turned the sheet of paper around and pushed it toward her friend.

"Okay. This is going to sound crazy, but just hear me out." Addie paused to collect her thoughts. "The night Aunt Kate was attacked, I couldn't sleep. I came down and made tea, and then, well, I guess I did a tea-leaf reading."

Chelsea looked up from the sheet of paper, her eyes brightening. She looked like she wanted to say something but instead allowed Addie to continue.

For the next several minutes, Addie described what'd happened—the visions, the voices, the weird physical sensations. Then she repeated what Betty had told her about the messages in the tea leaves.

"I didn't want to believe it," Addie said. "I didn't really even want to think about it. But then I decided to try to repeat the experiment." She explained how her second reading had given the exact same result. "And I tuned into the voices. They were saying, '*not dead, but not alive*' over and over."

Chelsea shivered visibly. Then she licked her lips and reached across the table to touch the back of Addie's hand.

"It's not crazy. Not at all," Chelsea said. A grin was beginning to spread over her face. She seemed almost jubilant, her eyes sparkling. "I always hoped this would happen."

Addie tilted her head. "What do you mean?"

"I knew you had a gift," Chelsea said. "I knew it back when we were teenagers. Your aunt wanted to start exploring it with you, but then after your parents wouldn't let you come that one summer, she stopped trying to teach you. It sounds like your parents had strong objections to her trying to train you in magic."

"Magic?" Addie repeated incredulously. "Let's not step off into the deep end."

Chelsea drew a breath and put on a patient expression. "Addie. This is a gift. You can't see that?"

Scrunching her face, Addie snorted softly. "It doesn't feel like a gift. It feels more like I'm losing it. I mean, how do you explain this phenomenon? Was I hallucinating? Was it something in the tea? Do I have a brain tumor? There has to be an explanation."

With a gentle laugh, Chelsea shook her head. "No, you don't have a tumor. You have an ability."

Addie looked down at the table as her conflicting emotions battled each other. She was a scientist. She prided herself on her intellect, on being able to explain the world using rational thought. Magic was the opposite of all of that.

Magic didn't *exist*.

"I don't think I can see it that way," she said quietly. "But I don't want to rule out anything that could lead me to Kate. Do you think we can set aside any talk of magic and gifts and abilities for the moment and try to figure out if there's something useful in my hallucinations?"

"Sure," Chelsea said.

Chapter Fourteen

IT WAS OBVIOUS CHELSEA WAS disappointed that Addie didn't want to talk about magical gifts, but she just couldn't stomach it. It was too much.

"I think the universe is trying to bring something very special fully into your life," Chelsea said carefully. "But you're not quite ready for it. So, let's just treat these pictures as clues and leave it at that for now."

Gratitude swept through Addie. "Thank you. I just want to find Kate and bring her home."

Chelsea pulled her phone from her slouchy bag. "I'm going to see if I can find a tasseography symbol directory online."

Tasseography? Addie suppressed a sigh. Putting a pseudo-scientific name to what had happened didn't make her feel better about it. But Chelsea was trying to be helpful.

"If it helps, I got the sense that these two images have to do with figuring out what happened to Kate." With her finger, Addie circled the drawings of the flower in the bottle and smiling face with the floating brain. "And I think the other two pertain specifically to the attacker."

"Oo, that's good," Chelsea said. "It's super important to listen to your instincts with this gi—I mean this thing you can do."

She'd nearly said "gifts," but Addie just couldn't bring herself to see it that way. Well, maybe if it brought Aunt Kate back. If it did, Addie would allow that the hallucinations had been useful and then do her best to forget they ever happened.

"Hm," Chelsea said after a few minutes. "I'm not sure about the smiling person with the floaty brain or the flower in the bottle. But the lightning bolt clearly symbolizes a rift between two people."

"Zelda's desire to buy the shop has definitely caused a rift between her and Kate," Addie said.

"So has Lisette's fury toward Kate," Chelsea said.

"You really think Lisette is still a strong suspect?"

"For sure," Chelsea said with certainty. "You saw her short fuse. It's, like, microscopic. And when she flies off the handle, things fly around the room. Violently."

Addie frowned. "I don't know. If Lisette had really thrown something at Kate, wouldn't we have seen evidence of that? The scene indicated that Kate hit her head on the corner of the counter. There weren't any objects that had obviously been thrown at her."

"What about the cash register?"

"It was tipped over, but it would have had blood on it if it'd hit Kate's head," Addie said. "And I think it would have landed closer to where I found her."

Chelsea tapped the piece of paper, her finger right next to the L with the knife underlining it. "L for Lisette. You said this was a clue about the attacker."

She really seemed to think Lisette had done it. But Addie couldn't help wondering if the personal history between Lisette and Chelsea was influencing her judgement.

"True," Addie allowed. "But it also could be for Larson. That's Zelda's last name. And the lightning bolt makes more sense with Zelda, too. She and Kate have been neighbors and friends for many years, until Zelda's recent push to buy this space. In the voicemails, there's a high degree of animosity from Zelda. That's a huge shift from how she used to be toward my aunt. In contrast, Lisette is a newcomer to the street, and I don't think she and Kate really knew each other as anything more than casual acquaintances. There wasn't really a relationship between them. Not like with Zelda."

Pressing her glossed lips together, Chelsea regarded the drawing. She didn't seem ready to concede that Zelda was a stronger suspect than Lisette. But Chelsea had been patient with Addie about all the magic nonsense, so she would give her friend the same courtesy.

"Hey," Chelsea said, looking up. "What if you tried another reading? Maybe thinking more specifically about the suspect this time?"

Addie shook her head. "I don't want to get any more caught up in this stuff than I already am. Besides, the facts should be the primary things to lead us to the guilty person, not . . ." She trailed off and waved her hand at the piece of paper.

"Okay, why don't we keep looking for interpretations of these symbols online?" Chelsea suggested. Her tone was neutral, but she avoided meeting Addie's gaze.

They searched for a while without much luck.

"Want to get something to eat?" Addie asked.

Chelsea glanced at her watch. "Actually, I think I'll just head home. I'm a little tired."

"Oh. Sure," Addie said. "And I'm sorry if my reaction to all of this mystical stuff offended you. I really didn't mean it as an attack on anything you believe in."

"I know." Chelsea's mouth tightened in what might have been an attempt at a smile.

"Thank you for everything, Chels," Addie said, following her friend downstairs.

"You're welcome, hon."

She let Chelsea out, checked the doors to make sure the shop was locked, and went back upstairs, where she poured Lucky a bowl of kibble.

But Addie wasn't in the mood to eat. She'd hurt Chelsea's feelings. It wasn't intentional. It was just a difference between the two of them. Still, Addie felt bad.

She sat down, flipped on the TV, and then pulled Kate's purse out of the paper bag. The paperwork for the sale of the shop's space to Zelda had gotten crumpled. Addie smoothed it over her leg.

She held Kate's phone for a moment, debating about whether to enter the code. Maybe Kate had tried to call it. Addie unlocked the device, but there were no new voice messages. Just a few inconsequential texts that appeared to be from friends or clients. Addie listened to Zelda's voicemails again in an attempt to confirm she hadn't been imagining what she'd heard.

Nope. If anything, Zelda sounded even more irate than Addie remembered.

Her stomach began to grumble, but she didn't feel like making anything. A burger from Grinning Catfish Brewery would really hit the spot, though.

Hopping up, she snapped on Lucky's leash, grabbed her purse and the shop key, and let herself out.

There was a truck parked in front of her car, and she recognized the back of the man leaning over into the bed.

"Hi, Trey," she called out.

He straightened, turned, and gave her a smile, brushing his hair out of his gray-green eyes.

He seemed like the type of guy who let his hair grow out between haircuts and was probably totally unaware of how stylish it looked. Addie had been too distraught the first couple of times they'd met, but now she recognized his chill vibe in the faded jeans, concert tee, and sneakers he wore. It was a brand of effortless attractiveness that tended to catch her eye. Her ex-fiancé Jeremy had the same sort of look.

"Hey, Addie," he said. "I've been meaning to stop by. I had to drive to Portland yesterday to pick up supplies for the shop remodel, and I ended up staying the night with some friends." His expression sobered. "Any word on your aunt?"

"We haven't caught the person who attacked her, and I still don't know where she is," Addie said. "Today I thought we'd caught the person, but the police followed up and her alibi was pretty good, so . . . back to the drawing board." She shrugged.

"I'm so sorry," he said.

"Hey, random question for you," Addie said as something occurred to her. "Have you ever seen Zelda Larson, the antique store owner, use a key to get into Wild Rose?"

Squinting, he slanted his gaze up and to the side. "Yeah, I have. One time on a Sunday, I came out and saw her letting herself in. We only exchanged a few words. She made a joke about having to get inside to turn off the alarm before the place exploded."

Addie's breath stilled. "She used a key and then turned off the alarm? You're sure?"

"Yep, positive."

On Thursday night, Zelda could have let herself in and waited until Kate showed up. The antique dealer was a tall, big-boned woman who easily could have overpowered Kate in a surprise attack. Would Zelda really try to murder her long-time neighbor just to get the shop space?

It seemed extreme, but . . . Zelda had been acting so strangely, and she was so fixated on getting her hands on Kate's space.

The pieces were sliding together.

"Addie? Are you okay?" Trey asked, peering into her eyes.

She gave her head a shake. "Uh, yeah, sorry I spaced out there for a second."

"I need to run by the hardware store before it closes, but let me know if you need anything."

She managed a smile. "Thank you. Good night."

Walking toward Grinning Catfish with Lucky in tow, Addie's thoughts whirled.

Zelda had motive—the shop. Her size gave her means. And having access to the key and security system code provided opportunity for her to lie in wait for Kate.

Plus, there was the L with the knife. And the two figures separated by lightning.

It was all there. And it all pointed squarely at Zelda.

Addie stopped on the corner in front of the bookstore and pulled out her phone, her finger poised to call Detective McCann. But she hesitated. The detective wouldn't be happy to have Addie presenting another suspect, especially so soon after the case against Georgia had collapsed and McCann had given Addie a final, stern warning.

She tucked her phone away. If she could get Zelda to confess to the crime and where Kate was, Addie could avoid more trouble with the officials on the case.

The antique shop was closed for the day, so Addie had missed her opportunity to confront Zelda. But it would be torture to wait until the next day. Maybe Bennett could use his P.I. skills to find Zelda's home address.

Addie's stomach rumbled like a thunderstorm threatening on the horizon. Dinner first, and then a call to Bennett. It wouldn't do to get lightheaded from low blood sugar while she was trying to persuade Zelda to confess to the attack.

At the brewery, Addie ordered dinner to go and took it back to Wild Rose, where she ate quickly. Then she called Bennett.

"Hi, it's Addie," she said. "I know it's after hours, but I was wondering if you could help me with something."

"Sure, I'll do my best. What's up?"

"I need Zelda Larson's home address. She's the one who attacked Kate. I would call the police, but Detective McCann definitely won't be receptive to another accusation from me, so I need to get Zelda to confess."

There was a beat of silence on the other line.

"Are you at Wild Rose?" Bennett asked.

"Yeah."

"I was just wrapping up at the office," he said. "Could I come by so we can talk about this in person? I can be there in ten minutes."

"Oh. Okay, thanks. I'll watch for you."

They hung up, and Addie went downstairs and sat on the stool behind the cash register with her elbows propped on the counter and her chin on her fist. Bennett had sounded less enthusiastic than Addie had expected. What was up with that?

When he appeared at the door, she went to let him in.

"Let's sit down and you can tell me about the case you've built," he said.

They sat across from each other at one of the café tables, and Addie recounted everything she'd come up with, minus the visions in the tea leaves.

"Opportunity, means, and motive," she said. "Pretty straightforward, don't you think?"

Bennett reached down to scratch Lucky behind the ear, seeming to mentally chew on what Addie had presented.

"You've got the basic pieces, for sure," he said. "But I don't think you should go to her home and confront her. She could get angry and violent."

"All the better if she did," Addie said. "That'd just strengthen the case against her."

"If she feels harassed, she could call the police, and well, it could all blow up on you." He leaned his forearms on the table, his dark eyes intent on her. "I get that you want to move on this now, but would you be willing to let me go talk to her tomorrow morning?"

Addie chewed her bottom lip as she fought the urge to argue against what he was proposing. He was sincerely trying to be helpful, and even protective.

"Look at it this way," he said. "If I go in a professional capacity, I'll get in less trouble than you will if you try to question her and she flies off the handle."

"I guess that's true," Addie said.

"All you have to do is hire me, say you want me to help you find your aunt. Looking for missing persons is the type of thing P.I.s do. McCann will have a harder time nailing us for interfering with the investigation of the attack, if that's the contractual agreement between me and you."

"I suppose that makes sense," Addie said. "What's your rate?"

"A buck."

Her brows shot up. "An hour?"

"Nope. Total. Give me a buck, and I'll draw up a contract."

A smile tugged at the corners of her lips. "You don't have to do that. I'll pay what you normally charge."

"Sorry, but that's my rate today. Take it or leave it." One side of his mouth quirked up, showing his dimple.

With a laugh, Addie pushed back her chair, stood, and went to her purse where she pulled a one-dollar bill from her wallet.

"Bennett, I really do want to repay you for all you've done," she said as she passed the cash to him.

"Let's find Kate, and then we'll worry about that," he said, taking the dollar.

He folded it in half, then in half again, and carefully tucked it into the pocket of his short-sleeve button down.

"Thank you, a hundred times over," she said.

"Thanks for hiring me," he said, giving her a wink. "Text me your email, and I'll get the contract sent over. Tomorrow, I'll go to the antique store first thing."

Addie let out a breath, surprised at her relief. Maybe it was a good idea to let someone else handle Zelda.

She walked him to the door and locked up. But she wasn't ready to settle down for the evening. There were still things she needed to look into.

Grabbing Lucky's leash, her purse, and keys, she turned to the little dog.

"Let's go on a drive to west Stargaze," she said.

He wagged and bounded to the front door, where he trotted in excited circles until she caught up.

Chapter Fifteen

WHEN ADDIE PULLED AWAY FROM Wild Rose Teas and Apothecary, the sun had just set. She flipped on the Ford's headlights and turned left at the end of the block.

Retracing the route she'd taken earlier, she ended up at Bowl of Plenty. The soup kitchen was dark and the lot empty, which she'd expected but she'd still wanted to check. She sat at the curb for a few minutes, hoping maybe someone was there working late—someone who knew Aunt Kate. But it appeared the staff had gone home for the day.

On the way to Bowl of Plenty, she'd seen a lot more people on the sidewalks around the apartment buildings than earlier in the day, which had piqued her curiosity. Doubling back, she intended to cruise through the streets that separated the apartment buildings.

But in the few minutes it'd taken to go to the soup kitchen and return to the residential area, barriers had been placed across the streets, preventing her from driving where she'd planned. She turned around and drove another couple of streets over to try from that direction.

More barriers. And all of them had signs that said things like "Restricted Area," "Keep Out After Dark," and "No Access Beyond This Point."

"What the—?" she muttered under her breath.

Squinting, she peered through the windshield, searching for some explanation for why the streets were blocked off. The headlights revealed plenty of people moving around on the next block. And was that a bonfire in the street and the faint thump of music?

Maybe there was a block party or some other neighborhood event. If that was the case, then why the unwelcoming signage?

A rap on her window nearly sent her jumping out of her skin. She swiveled her head to find a man standing next to the car. Lucky started growling.

"You can't get through here tonight," he said. "You'll have to turn around."

He wore a faint polite smile, but his eyes were bloodshot and his skin looked . . . greenish? Or maybe that was just the dim lighting.

"Shush, Lucky," she stage-whispered at the dog, but he continued to let out low warning rumbles.

Addie cracked her window open a couple of inches, furtively checking to make sure the doors were locked.

"What's going on in there?" she asked the man.

"It's a private event," he said. He pointed to one of the signs. "No access tonight. Please turn around and go back the way you came, miss."

She caught a whiff of what she thought was roasting meat. "Is it a neighborhood barbecue?"

"No. Please be on your way."

His smile had faded, and his bloodshot eyes stared at her with an intensity that gave her the creepy-crawlies.

"Uh, okay," she said.

It took a three-point turn to get the Ford aimed the other direction, and the man stood with his arms crossed, watching her progress. He was still there in the rearview mirror as she drove away. When she turned the corner, Lucky finally stopped growling.

"You know what?" she said, glancing back at the dog. "We're not going home. We came here for answers, and we're going to get some."

She made several rounds of the neighborhood, gaining an idea of the perimeter of the restricted area and trying to check it out from every angle. The darker it got, the more active the party—or whatever it was—seemed to become. Finding a place to park that was well away from any of the people stationed at the barriers, she shut off the lights and killed the engine.

Then she turned to the back seat. "Okay, Lucky, here's the deal. We're going to have to be sneaky. But if we get caught, we need to look like we belong there. Make sense?"

He gave her a doggy grin and thumped his tail.

"Oh," she added. "And on the chance you do actually understand what I'm saying, we want to be on the lookout for anything that might help us find Aunt Kate. She's the one who owns the place where we've been staying, so you should know what she smells like."

He yipped and put his front paws up on the arm rest of the back door.

When she went to let him out, he hopped down before she realized his leash had somehow come off his collar.

"Hey, wait just a minute, little guy," she said.

But when she went toward him with the leash, he dodged out of the way. After a couple more tries, she blew out an exasperated breath. She didn't have time to play tag with him all night.

"You do seem like you know how to handle yourself," she said. "Don't mess up, or it's leash city from now on, okay?"

He pranced in a circle, which made her grin.

She returned the leash to the back seat, locked the car, and made sure the small can of pepper spray she usually carried was in her small cross-body purse.

With adrenaline putting a spring in her step and her heart tapping in anticipation, she set out toward the blocked-off area.

Going slowly at first, she kept to the shadows. All the streetlamps seemed to be out of order in this neighborhood, but she'd been right about the bonfire. In fact, there were a few of them spaced out every block or so. And it definitely seemed like a party. Music was playing, and people were milling around, laughing, and chatting.

It looked like a normal mix of people in a neighborhood, except for one thing—there were no children. Maybe alcohol was being served and that was why kids weren't allowed.

She still didn't see any barbecues, even though the aroma of a cookout grew stronger the closer she got to the edge of the event.

"Okay, boy, remember. Sniff around for Aunt Kate," Addie whispered.

Trying to look casual, she strolled around a corner and aimed for the heart of the restricted area, determined to get a good look around and see if Lucky picked up on anything.

At first, no one seemed to take much notice of her. But as she got deeper into the crowd, more gazes swung her way. When she was close enough to one of the bonfires to see the faces in the light, something struck her. Everyone there had very bloodshot eyes. And the green pallor she'd noticed on the man who'd told her to leave hadn't been her imagination, either. Everyone there had skin the color of the snow peas her mother used to grow in the vegetable garden.

And the crowd wasn't just glancing at her. They were following her with glazed, penetrating stares that sent a shiver up her spine. The sudden urge to get away had her wheeling around, ready to scoot back to her car, and looking for Lucky. But the crowd had thickened, and people were blocking her way.

Sidestepping around them, she muttered "excuse me" and tried to weave through. But more and more people were turning her way and drifting toward her. And even more eerie, the laughter and talking in her immediate vicinity had ceased. With wide eyes and twitching nostrils, the crowd pushed in.

Addie's heart started to pound. What on earth was happening?

"Move, please," she said, elbowing her way through the bodies that started to blur together in her field of vision. "I need to get through."

She leaned forward, forcing her way past people who appeared strangely dazed.

Just as the edge of the crowd was within sight, a hand closed around her arm. Addie whipped around, coming face-to-face with a woman in a pink sundress and a blond bob. She was leering at Addie, and oh no . . . was that drool dripping from the corner of her mouth?

Addie grimaced and tried to recoil, but the woman tightened her grip.

"Nooo, don't gooo," the woman groaned.

Panic twisted Addie's insides. She jerked her arm away so forcefully she stumbled backward and crashed into someone. Hands were reaching toward her.

She scrambled on all fours through the forest of legs. Then Lucky was there, snarling and barking his sweet little head off. That distracted the people around Addie enough that she could slip past, freeing herself from the throng.

She got to her feet and was just about to break into a run when a man lunged at her. She tried to spring away, but the man clipped her foot and she went sprawling, her hands and bare knees hitting the sandy asphalt.

Wincing at the sharp pain of fresh road rash, she kicked out, trying to free her foot.

"Let go!" screeched.

Lucky was bouncing back and forth, barking furiously.

And then someone was there, pulling her to her feet.

"Run, Addie," Bennett commanded.

He held her hand tightly and pulled her hard, forcing her into a sprint to keep up with him.

"Go, Lucky!" she shouted back over her shoulder, and to her relief saw the little dog bound after them.

They sprinted hard for two blocks, and then Bennett pointed ahead and to the right. "My car's up there."

By the time they reached the Jeep Sahara parked on the curb, Addie was too breathless to speak.

Bennett helped her into the passenger seat, lifted Lucky onto her lap, and slammed the door. She watched him run around to the driver's side. Just as he started the engine, a dozen men and women came around the corner into view. They weren't moving quickly, but the way they walked was . . . eerie. A shambling kind of shuffle. Addie shivered, watching their clumsy, loose-limbed movements.

Bennett stepped on the gas, speeding away.

"My car is that way," she said, pointing to the left.

He shook his head. "We're going to have to leave it there for now. I'll bring you back to get it tomorrow."

She stared at him, wide-eyed. "Why can't we get it now?"

"It's not safe," he said, his eyes on the road.

"How did you know I was there?" she asked.

"I saw you drive west from my office window," he said. "I had a hunch you might be out looking for trouble tonight. I caught up with you just in time."

"What was wrong with those people?" Addie asked, her throat dry and her pulse still racing uncomfortably.

"That's . . . a little hard to explain."

"Bennett, I really need you to tell me," she said, her voice quiet but urgent.

He gave her a grim look. "Looks like I have no choice after what you did out there. But Addie, they know you've seen them, and that means you're in danger."

"But they don't know who I am," she protested. She twisted around to look behind them. "And no one's following me."

"They got your scent. That's all they need to find you, if they decide they want to."

A shiver wound up Addie's spine. "My scent?" she whispered.

"Let's get somewhere safe, and then I'll tell you who what's going on."

Instead of driving to Wild Rose, he pulled up in front of his office building.

"I've got security cameras mounted outside," he said. "We'll know if anyone tries to track you here."

Track her? Addie's hands went cold.

He came around to her side. "Carry Lucky," he said.

And taking her arm, he hurried her to the door, where he quickly unlocked the heavy deadbolt. A hand on her elbow guided her inside while he looked back over his shoulder. He locked the door and then flipped on the lobby light.

"Let's go upstairs where we can sit down," he said.

Once inside his office, he turned on his desk lamp, leaving the overhead lighting off. The folding chair where Georgia had sat was still there, and Addie sank heavily onto it. Lucky jumped off her lap and stood next to her.

Bennett eased into his chair and leaned his forearms on the desk, looking down for a moment as he seemed to collect his thoughts.

When he looked up, his eyes were grave. "When you asked me if there was a leper colony in Stargaze, you weren't totally out in left field."

Addie swallowed hard, nodding for him to go on.

"The folks you ran headlong into tonight, they're, well, some might call them zombies."

She blinked. Then she frowned. "Don't tease me, Bennett."

"I'm not," he said quietly.

They just stared at each other for a long, silent minute.

"What, exactly, do you mean by zombies?" she asked slowly.

"The condition happens when a healthy person is bitten by one of them. There's a transformation that happens. Once it's complete, the person becomes one of *them*. They go through cycles of hunger, feeding, and then falling into a semi-catatonic state."

"Feeding? Feeding on what?" Addie asked, dreading the answer.

"Brain matter."

She recoiled with a cringe.

"They prefer to call themselves Shufflers, for the way they move when they're catatonic," he said. "Some refer to them as the Reanimated. Others just call them monsters. Or worse."

"Reanimated," Addie repeated. "Does that mean they—they die before they become . . ." She trailed off, unable to bring herself to say the word zombies. Or even Shufflers.

He gave a small nod. "Death is part of the process. And that's why they don't consider themselves fully human. Reasoning is, a human doesn't recover from death."

She squeezed her eyes closed for a moment, trying to make sense of it all. It was crazy, too crazy to believe. Except . . . well, she'd seen them. And those people at the block party weren't *right*.

"It's a lot, I know," he said. "It's pretty wild."

"But it's true? You know with one-hundred-percent certainty that this is real?"

"I do."

"And you said my aunt is friends with them?" Addie asked.

He nodded. "They have human allies. Friends. They need people to help them source food."

Brains. Ugh.

Addie tried not to let her mouth twist in distaste. "Does the food have to be of human origin?"

"Yep. Only human brains will do the trick. But they don't want to murder for their food, so they have a sort of secret supply chain. They get brains from medical research facilities. Morgues. Places of that nature."

"Chelsea told me about tourists who disappeared years ago," Addie said. "Were they victims of the, uh, Shufflers?"

"Some of them were, unfortunately, but that was back before they got their supply chain in order," Bennett said.

Addie sagged back in her chair and let out a long breath. She didn't want to ask, but she had to.

"You thought these Shufflers might have had something to do with what happened to Kate," Addie said. "Do you think they hurt her?"

"It's possible. But it's also possible that she may have, well, joined them."

Addie's throat went dry. All she could do was stare at him wide-eyed as the image from the tea leaves, the little picture of the happy woman with a brain floating above her, resurfaced.

"Maybe . . . maybe you're right," she said. "Bennett, there's something I think I should tell you about. Something that happened to me recently. It's not quite as insane as zombies, but it's not far off."

Chapter Sixteen

BENNETT COCKED HIS HEAD CURIOUSLY.

"Something almost as insane as zombies?" he asked with a mildly amused lilt in his voice.

"Yeah," Addie said.

She told him about the tea leaves. Every detail.

"The little smiling face with the brain made no sense until now," she said. "But I think that's Kate, and the brain symbolizes that she's one of them now."

"That lines up," he said.

"I think there's someone who knows for sure," Addie said. She recounted her run-in with Betty outside Bowl of Plenty. "I think she was taking things to Kate. Or maybe dropping them off so someone else could take them."

"Hm, it's possible," Bennett said. "But from what I know, it's too soon for Kate to be completely through the transition. She wouldn't yet be in a state where she'd need those kinds of supplies."

"Maybe Betty was leaving them for when Kate would need them." Addie shook her head. "Either way, if this is true, that means my aunt is alive."

"Well, alive-*ish*," Bennett said with the barest twitch of a grin.

Addie tried for a smile, but it faltered as her eyes filled instead.

"I'm sorry," she said. "I don't mean to get emotional. I just really, really want to believe that Aunt Kate isn't dead."

He reached into the drawer with the tissues, pulled one out, and offered it.

"It's okay," he said. "Don't be embarrassed."

She dabbed at the corners of her eyes. "I'm not usually like this, I swear. It's been a heck of a few days. I think it's catching up with me."

"I'd be upset, too, in your place. Learning all of this. Worrying about Kate."

Giving a little laugh, Addie shook her head. "Oh, you don't even know. This isn't even the half of it. My life had pretty much imploded before I got to Stargaze." She waved her hand. "But that's not anything we need to get into right now."

"I do appreciate your confidence, Addie," Bennett said. "You telling me about the tea-leaf reading means a lot."

"Right, that," she said ruefully. "Thank you for not laughing in my face."

"You're not alone, you know," he said. "There are others with abilities around here."

She closed her eyes. "Oh no, you sound like Chelsea."

When she opened her eyes, she found Bennett's face was closed off, his gaze focused off to the side.

"I should probably get you home, don't you think?" he asked, pushing back his chair. "It's getting pretty late, and you've probably had enough excitement for one night."

Shoot. She'd said the wrong thing. He'd been about to tell her something, but she'd preemptively pooh-poohed it.

"Bennett, if there's something you wanted to say . . ."

"Nah, it was nothing," he said, forcing a smile. "Ready to go?"

She decided not to press right then. "Sure."

"I know it's only a block away, but I'm going to drive you to Wild Rose just to be safe," he said. "It goes without saying, but keep your doors locked after dark. The Shufflers settle down and go inside at dawn."

Addie picked up Lucky, and the three of them went outside and got into Bennett's car. He drove around the corner, parked in her usual spot on Pine Avenue, and then walked in with her to do a quick sweep of the shop and the apartment.

"I'm going to speak to Zelda Larson first thing like we talked about," he said. "Then I'll take you to get your car."

"Sounds like a good plan," Addie said. "And again, I can't thank you enough for everything you've done. Especially for pulling me out of a scrape tonight."

"You're welcome, Addie."

He turned to go, and she took a couple of steps after him. "Wait, Bennet? Would the Shufflers have killed me if you hadn't shown up?"

When he faced her, the look in his eyes gave her a little chill. "They could have. Usually there are monitors roaming the area to make sure nothing gets out of hand, but they can't be everywhere at once."

"That's scary," Addie said in a low voice. "Thank you again. Good night."

She locked up after him and trudged upstairs.

Wow, what a day. Zombies, and tea leaves, and suspects, oh my.

She looked down at Lucky. "I don't know about you, buddy, but I need to crash. My poor brain needs a chance to process all of this."

Brain.

A brain that might have become zombie food if Bennett hadn't shown up.

She shut off the shop lights, and Lucky followed her upstairs. Ten minutes later, they were both asleep on the daybed.

THE NEXT MORNING, ADDIE GOT ready for the day and then sat down with a cup of coffee and a buttered English muffin. She sent a text to Bennett letting him know he was welcome to have his morning coffee with her instead of picking it up at La Petite Patisserie while he waited for Zelda's A to Z Antiques to open. Not that Addie was trying to get him to stop patronizing Lisette's café. It was just an offer to save him a few bucks and have some company.

When twenty minutes passed and Bennett didn't respond, Addie didn't think much of it. He'd planned to speak to Zelda first thing, and the antique store should have opened about ten minutes ago.

Not knowing how long it would take to question the antique shop owner, Addie busied herself around Wild Rose, using Kate's feather duster to go over the shelves and straightening all the bottles and jars.

Upstairs, Addie went through the fridge, tossing out half a turkey sub Kate had left that was starting to look squishy and a few expired yogurt containers. Addie straightened the rest of the contents and started a list of items she would pick up at the grocery store. After putting away the dishes that had dried on the rack next to the sink, vacuuming the small living room, and feeding Lucky, she glanced at the time and was surprised to find over an hour had passed since she'd texted Bennett.

Could he still be at Zelda's?

She started to send another message but then deleted it. They'd talked about their plans. He'd show up when he was able.

Instead, she sent a text to Chelsea, asking if she wanted to meet up for lunch. So much had happened since they'd seen each other. How much could Addie disclose? Would Chelsea be in danger if she learned about the Shufflers?

Addie couldn't see keeping such huge news from her friend. Especially when the information could very well lead to Kate.

Gazing through the front window, Addie's eyes rested on Betty's emporium. The mystic had to know about the Shufflers. Was she a friend of the community like Kate was? Whether yes or no, in hindsight it seemed obvious that Betty knew Kate was with them, or at least suspected it.

"My aunt is with zombies," Addie whispered, trying to wrap her head around it.

But was Kate there as a victim or as one of them?

Betty wouldn't have been taking supplies to Kate if she'd become zombie food. And, Addie's tea-leaf reading indicated Kate was alive. Correction: not alive, but also not dead.

Alive-ish, as Bennett had said.

As Addie went around the apartment and the shop emptying trash cans into a large garbage bag, she tried to silently reassure herself that Aunt Kate was out there somewhere, relatively okay. There was good evidence supporting that assumption. Well, if she considered things like tea-leaf readings and voices in her head evidence.

Addie tied off the trash bag and left it near the back door, intending to take it out later.

Chelsea texted saying she'd come to Wild Rose at eleven forty-five and they could walk somewhere for lunch.

But there was still nothing from Bennett.

Addie called him and after several rings got his voicemail. She left a quick message, trying not to sound concerned. Then she went to the window and looked down the road. She could see part of Bennett's office building, but not the front where his car might be parked.

Curiosity got the best of her. She snapped on Lucky's leash, locked Wild Rose, and went down to the end of the block. She glanced into Zelda's and saw only one person inside—a tall woman with her back turned, who must have been a customer, though something about her struck Addie as vaguely familiar. Zelda was nowhere in sight. Maybe Bennett was talking to her in the small office on the upper floor of the antique store.

Addie and Lucky trotted across the street, quickly scooting past Lisette's café, until they stood next to the auto repair shop. The vantage point gave Addie a full view of the street in front of Bennett's office. His car wasn't there.

Frowning, Addie retraced her steps. He hadn't parked near Zelda's, either.

Maybe he'd decided to investigate Aunt Kate's whereabouts instead of questioning Zelda.

Addie's heart leapt at the thought that Kate might return soon.

Back inside Wild Rose, Addie paced. She still had an hour until lunch, but nothing to occupy herself, and she was antsy about Bennett's silence.

Finally, she couldn't take it any longer. She needed something useful to do. If Bennett was in west Stargaze working on bringing

Aunt Kate home, the least Addie could do was accomplish something here.

Leaving Lucky napping on the daybed, she slipped out of the shop with her pepper spray in the pocket of her jacket and turned left toward the antique store.

Through the door, she spotted Zelda moving a gilded frame. With a deep breath, Addie reached for the door handle.

The antique proprietor looked up and leaned the frame against a chest of drawers when she saw Addie. The older woman's face tightened.

Staying near the door, with twenty feet between her and Zelda, Addie cleared her throat.

"Hi, Zelda. Has a man named Bennett been here to speak with you this morning?"

Zelda's forehead wrinkled. "Bennett? I . . . I don't think so. But I'm not having a very good day."

Addie tilted her head. "What's wrong?"

"I'm just forgetful." Zelda blinked several times. "Who is this Bennett person?"

"Oh, just a friend of mine," Addie said. She cautiously moved a few steps closer. "Zelda, do you have a key to Wild Rose?"

"Yes, of course I do," she said. "Kate gave it to me for emergencies years ago."

"And she probably gave you the security code for the alarm system, too, right?" Addie asked.

"Sure, I have it written down in the office," Zelda said.

"When was the last time you used the key to get into Kate's store?"

Zelda's eyes lost focus, and she began glancing around her, as if the answer lay nearby. "Um . . . I think maybe I used it a few weeks back? Or maybe it wasn't that long ago."

"What about more recently?" Addie asked. Her heart was beginning to tap more rapidly. "Maybe late at night, when it was dark out?"

Zelda straightened. "Oh! Oh, yes. I did use it at night. I remember fumbling around a bit to find the keypad for the alarm."

"When?" Addie pressed. "What day was it? This past Thursday?"

"I don't—I don't know." Zelda shook her head. She squinted, seeming to think about it, and then her gaze sharpened. "That was the night Kate disappeared, wasn't it? And then you came here and yelled at me about her phone."

"What? I certainly didn't yell at you." Addie was sensing the conversation was beginning to unravel, as the older woman had started muttering under her breath. Addie had to raise her voice to get Zelda's attention. "Did you use your key to get into Wild Rose that night? Did you hurt Kate, Zelda?"

The older woman's face had gone red. "Stop it! Stop accusing me of things! Can't you see I'm having a bad day?"

Addie clenched her hands into fists at her sides, her heart starting to pound. "Well, you know what? Kate is probably having a much worse day than you are. Did you attack her because she wouldn't take your offer? Just tell me the truth."

"Get out," Zelda hollered hoarsely. "Get out of here now! I'm going to call the police!"

She marched over to the phone mounted on the wall and yanked the receiver to her ear. She punched 911 onto the keypad.

Addie's eyes popped wide. Oh, no. Zelda was serious about the police.

"Zelda, calm down," Addie said, but the antique dealer ignored her, instead shouting into the phone.

Well, one thing was clear. Not only had Addie failed to get a confession, she'd thoroughly lost control of the situation. She turned and hurried out of the antique store and back to Wild Rose, where she sprinted upstairs and dropped onto the daybed, her head in her hands.

Lucky sat next to her and licked her wrist.

"What a mess," Addie moaned. "Bennett is going to be mad. And Detective McCann—oh, fudgesicles. If she catches wind of this, it's really over for me."

She jumped when her phone rang. Maybe it was Bennett. She yanked the device from her pocket and read Chelsea's name on the caller ID.

"Hi, Chels," Addie answered.

"Hey, are you ready for lunch? I was just about to leave the boutique."

"Uh, yeah, but don't come to Wild Rose," Addie said. "I'll meet you on the other side of the block near Slice of Pie, okay?"

"Oh, all right. Is something wrong?"

"Yeah, but it can wait. I'll see you in a minute."

Feeling utterly deflated and more than a little paranoid that McCann would come pounding on the door at any second, Addie slipped out the back into the alley, rounded the corner, and then headed toward Slice of Pie.

Chelsea spotted Addie trudging down the sidewalk and came to meet her.

"Okay, something is definitely wrong," Chelsea said. "Your aura looks like the stink scribbles around Pigpen in the Snoopy cartoons."

Addie snorted. "Gee, thanks."

Chelsea pointed across the street at a sandwich shop. "Let's go there. They've got gluten-free bread, and their tuna melt is seriously amazing."

They crossed over to Gourmet Sammie, went in, and placed their orders at the counter. Addie took Chelsea's recommendation and got a tuna melt on house-made rye.

While they waited for the food, Addie told her friend about the events of the morning.

"I think I royally screwed things up," Addie said, her forehead falling onto her palms. "Zelda actually called the police on me. They're probably looking for me right now."

"What's she going to do, though? File a complaint? Probably the worst she could do is try to get a restraining order, and I doubt she'd get it."

Addie looked up in horror. "I didn't even think of that. Oh my gosh, that would be so humiliating." Her face heated at the thought of getting slapped with an order like she was a common criminal.

"I'm actually more concerned about Bennett," Chelsea said. "You know him better than I do, but I'm guessing it's unlike him to go silent like this."

"Yeah, it is," Addie said. She took out her phone and flipped to texts and calls, just to make sure she hadn't missed him. "I'm worried, too."

Their sandwiches arrived, but Addie's stomach was too balled up to eat more than half of hers.

"Hey, speaking of Bennett, I wanted to ask you something," Addie said, remembering the conversation Bennett had cut short the previous night. "Does he have some kind of special ability, like your aura thing?"

Chelsea's chewing slowed. She swallowed, set down her sandwich, and brushed the crumbs off her fingers. "I'm not sure he'd want me talking about it."

"It came up when the two of you were at Wild Rose chatting, right?" Addie asked, trying to ignore the less-than-comfortable feeling of being left out of a secret.

Chelsea nodded.

"How did you end up on the topic?"

"I sensed it," Chelsea said. "I can feel or sometimes even see in a person's aura when they're special like that. I felt it in Lisette back when we were kids, though I didn't understand what it was at the time. I saw it in Bennett. And . . . in you."

"You don't have to tell me if you don't think he'd want you to," Addie said. She wasn't quite ready to probe deeper into what Chelsea had observed about Addie's supposed ability.

"I think he might want you to know," Chelsea said. "But it'd be better if I let him tell you."

Addie waited quietly, looking out the window, while Chelsea finished her sandwich.

They were just getting up to go when Addie's phone rang.

It was Bennett.

"Are you okay? Where have you been?" she asked.

"I'm in the hospital," he said.

Chapter Seventeen

ADDIE GASPED. "OH NO! ARE you hurt?"

"I'm a little roughed up, yeah," Bennett said. It sounded like he was speaking through clenched teeth.

"It's got to be more than a little if you're at the hospital." Addie started waving at Chelsea, who widened her eyes when Addie mentioned the hospital. Addie pointed to the door.

They exited Gourmet Sammies and moved off to the side to stay out of the way of customers coming and going.

"What happened?" Addie asked.

"Someone jumped me from the back when I was going into the office this morning. Knocked me out just as I got into the lobby. When I came to, I was on the floor. Whoever did it kicked me around while I was out. Got a cracked rib or two."

Addie's hand flew to her mouth. "Oh, Bennett, you poor thing, that's horrible. Do you have any idea who the attacker was?"

"Not really. Before I got beaned in the head, the guy said, 'Stop investigating me. This is your one and only warning.' But I didn't recognize the voice."

"What can I do?" Addie asked.

"Well, I could really use a ride home," he said. "I'm free to go, but I'm a little woozy on pain meds at the moment."

"Of course," Addie said. "Chelsea and I can come and get you."

She looked at Chelsea questioningly, who nodded and pointed ahead. They started walking that way.

"Speaking of cars," Addie said into the phone. "I was looking for yours this morning. You say you made it to the office, but I didn't see your car in front."

"I parked a couple of blocks away," Bennett said. "It was a precaution in case the Shufflers happened to follow our trail. Unlikely, but I didn't want to lead them right to your doorstep by putting my car around the corner from Wild Rose."

"Oh, that was thoughtful," Addie said, realizing she hadn't gotten the chance to tell Chelsea about the zombies. "I thought maybe you'd gone to look for Kate."

"I might have avoided getting the tar kicked out of me if I had," he said with a small laugh followed by a groan.

"Which hospital are you at?" Addie asked.

Bennett gave her the name and directions, and they disconnected.

Chelsea's car turned out to be a brand new, adorable pale-yellow VW beetle convertible, which couldn't have been more fitting. There wouldn't be much room for a third passenger, but Addie could squeeze in the back and let Bennett sit up front.

"Someone attacked him, but he doesn't know who," Addie said as Chelsea pulled out of the lot where her bug was parked.

Addie filled her in while they drove.

"That's just terrible," Chelsea said. "Do you think it was related to Kate's attack and disappearance or one of Bennett's other clients?"

"That's a good question. I didn't think to ask," Addie said, realizing she'd assumed it had something to do with her aunt. But of course Bennett had other cases, too.

The hospital was only a ten-minute drive away, and Addie spotted his Jeep Sahara in the lot outside the emergency entrance. She felt terrible he'd driven himself to the E.R. Why hadn't he called her?

He was sitting in the nearly empty waiting area, and Addie's heart sank when she caught sight of the state he was in. There was a bandage wrapped around his head like a runner's headband, which probably meant he had stitches in his scalp. His button-down shirt had been ripped open, and there was blood on the shoulder.

Addie ran up to him. "Oh my gosh, you poor thing."

He leaned forward, wincing, and stood carefully. "It's not as bad as it looks," he said. "Nothing's broken, just cracked."

"Does it hurt?" Chelsea said.

"Deep breaths are a bit of a challenge, and I've got a rager of a headache, but I'll be fine," he said.

"Why don't you let me drive you in your car?" Addie suggested. "Chelsea's VW bug is a tight fit, and that way we can get your car back to your house."

"Can't argue with that logic," he said, and managed a small smile.

"I'll be right behind you," Chelsea said.

Addie followed Bennett's directions into the area of Stargaze that was northeast of downtown. It was an older neighborhood, but the houses were charming.

On the way, she confessed to her missteps with Zelda that morning.

"She called the actual police on me," Addie said miserably. "I'm so sorry I jumped the gun. I never should have gone over there. What if I go back to Wild Rose and they're waiting for me?"

"Want my advice?" Bennett asked.

She nodded.

"If they try to get you to come into the station, don't go," he said.

"Won't that tick off Detective McCann?"

"Probably, but I don't think you should let them corner you because it might just make things worse. They have no grounds for arrest, so you don't have to go in. Just steer clear of Zelda so you don't give her more ammo to use against you."

"Okay," she said and took a deep breath. "Thank you."

He pointed at a stucco house with steeply peaked roof lines and a neat, bright-green lawn in front.

She pulled to the curb and shut off the engine.

"Do you want me to come in with you?" she asked, casting a curious look at the front door. It would be interesting to get a glimpse into his personal space.

"Nah, the place is kind of a mess," he said. "But thank you."

Addie doubted his house was messy, if his neat, spare office or spotless car were any indication. Maybe he was just a private man.

"Is there anything I can bring you?" she asked.

"I'm good," he said. "I really just need to rest."

"Bennett, we have to find out who did this to you. You reported the attack to the police, right?"

"I didn't," he said. "I want to pull the footage from the security camera at the office and have a look, first."

Her brows shot up. "I totally forgot about the camera. How long will it take to do that?"

"Not long," he said.

"Will you call me as soon as you've reviewed it?"

"Sure will."

He looked like he really needed to sit down, so Addie handed him the car key.

"Was the attack related to Kate's case?" she asked.

He shook his head and then winced. "I'm not sure. Could be. But I've got a few other clients, so someone related to one of those contracts might have gone off the rails."

She let out a breath. "You'll be safe here, right?"

He gave her a little grin. "You offering your protection?"

"I guess that wouldn't be much help," she said sheepishly.

"It's a sweet offer. But I'll be fine. I've got a couple of guns in the house, if anyone tries to mess with me."

"Okay. But will you give me a call in a bit no matter what? Just so I know you're doing all right."

"I will, promise."

She watched him walk gingerly toward his door for a moment and then went and got into the yellow bug idling at the curb.

"The two of you seemed to have a lot to say to each other," Chelsea said with an arched brow.

Addie lifted a shoulder. "I just wanted to make sure he was going to be okay." She straightened. "Oh, Chels, I didn't even get to tell you about what happened last night. You're not going to believe this."

She launched into the story of going into west Stargaze, the cordoned-off area, the crazy encounter with the crowd at the block party, and Bennett swooping in to get her out. And everything Bennett had told her afterward.

Chelsea pulled to a stop at a light and swiveled her head to stare at Addie.

"Zombies?" Chelsea asked in a high-pitched voice. "Actual *zombies*?"

Addie nodded. "I know. It's crazy. Is it wrong that I kind of like being able to talk about something that's unbelievable to you for a change?"

The car behind them honked, and Chelsea stepped on the gas. She stared through the front windshield, shaking her head slowly. "I like to think I'm open-minded, but this is nuttier than a Costco-sized jar of crunchy Jiff."

"No kidding," Addie said. "If I wouldn't have seen it myself, I wouldn't believe one shred of it."

"You think they have Kate?"

"Possibly. I know it sounds weird, but I hope so," Addie said. "Because if they have her, and they're not, you know, feasting on her gray matter, then that means she's alive. Or, alive-*ish*, as Bennett says. I'd much rather that than losing her forever."

"Maybe we should go get your car," Chelsea suggested.

"Might as well. It's full daylight, so we should be safe. Bennett said after dawn the Shufflers settle down and aren't aggressive."

"You seem pretty comfortable with this whole idea of zombies," Chelsea remarked as she turned down Main Street.

"Not comfortable. Far from comfortable. But I can't deny what I saw, and I don't think Bennett is lying to me." She paused, collecting her thoughts. "You know, all this time I assumed that whoever attacked her also knew where she was. But now I'm thinking those are two totally separate events. I'm just not sure yet how they happened."

When they got to Pine Avenue, Addie glanced down the street and then groaned. Detective McCann's sedan was parked in front of Wild Rose, and the red-haired woman stood at the glass with her hands cupped around her eyes, peering inside.

"Oh, no, maybe Zelda is going to press charges after all," Addie said, her stomach plummeting at the thought of having her rights read to her. "Bennett actually told me not to go into the station unless they arrest me. And he said they didn't have grounds to do that."

"You'll just have to hide out, then," Chelsea said. "You're welcome to stay with me."

"That's nice of you, but I really feel like I should stay at Wild Rose."

"In case Kate shows up?" Chelsea asked.

"Yeah."

"But even if she does come home, her attacker still needs to be punished," Chelsea said.

"Absolutely."

"Still think it was Zelda?"

"Honestly, I haven't ruled her out." Addie's phone rang, and a glance at the caller I.D. made her groan again. "Ugh, it's Detective McCann." She tapped the Ignore button.

"I think later we should go over the suspect list again," Chelsea said. "Reevaluate each person."

"I appreciate your enthusiasm, Chels. Now that I'm really in the doghouse with McCann, I can't go poking around and asking questions. All I need is someone else deciding I'm harassing them. I'm not giving up, not by a long shot, but I'm going to have to be extra careful."

Addie gave directions to where the Ford Escape had been left. They drove past the areas where blockades had blocked off streets, and Addie couldn't help staring. The barriers and signs were gone, the streets and sidewalks were empty, and there was no sign of what had taken place the previous night.

She shivered. Even though the sun shone brightly, it still felt eerie.

"Do you happen to sense anything energy-wise here?" Addie asked.

"I'd have to get out and walk around to pick up any energetic vibrations."

Addie shuddered. "I don't recommend wandering these streets."

They reached her car, and she dashed out, jumped in, and slammed the button for the power locks like she was being chased by a pack of rabid wolves. It was silly to be so paranoid, but the previous night's experience had left an impression, and her pulse didn't settle until she was well away from that part of Stargaze.

Back on Pine Avenue, she nearly parked in front of Wild Rose out of habit but didn't want to tip off the authorities that she was there. She'd have to find a spot out of sight of the tea shop and then use the back door. Running from the law sure was inconvenient.

She called Chelsea and explained the parking situation. "Meet me in the alley, and we'll go in that way."

After leaving her car on the far side of the block mostly taken up by Grinning Catfish Brewery, Addie made her way back to the alley. Chelsea was waiting at Wild Rose's back door, and Addie used her key to get them inside.

Lucky came bounding down from upstairs, and Addie bent down to give his neck a scratch.

"Normally I'd say we could sit down here and have some tea, but I'd better stay upstairs and out of sight," Addie said.

They went up and settled at Kate's little dining table, and Chelsea took out her sparkly notebook and purple pen while Addie heated up the coffee that was left in the pot and then filled two mugs. Tea sounded better, but the thought of tea leaves made her uneasy.

"Okay, here's where we left off," Chelsea said, looking down at her notebook. "Lisette and Enzo in the suspect column, and Zelda in the person-of-interest column."

Addie propped her elbows on the table and inhaled the fragrant steam rising from her mug. "Wow, a lot has happened since then."

"No kidding. I assume you want to move Zelda over to suspects?"

Addie nodded. "And even though Georgia was cleared by the police, something about her is still sticking in my mind. It was just so odd that she was the one to return Kate's notebook."

"Person of interest?" Chelsea suggested.

"Sure." Addie sighed. "The list is bigger than it was before. I really thought this would be more straightforward, you know?"

"What if I ran over to Slice of Pie and spoke to Enzo?" Chelsea asked. "He likes attention from girls. I bet I could get him to talk about the plane ticket and how he got the money to pay for it."

"Why not? If it means we can eliminate a suspect, that would at least be a step in the right direction."

After watching long and hard to make sure no one was staking out Wild Rose Teas and Apothecary, Chelsea left out the front to go to Slice of Pie. Feeling like an animal scurrying back into the shadows, Addie retreated up to the apartment.

When her phone rang and Bennet's name lit up the screen, she pounced on the device.

"Did you figure out who attacked you?" she asked eagerly.

Chapter Eighteen

BENNETT MADE A SOUND THAT was half-laugh, half-grunt. "I've got footage, but I'll tell you right off the bat I can't clearly identify him. He's about my height, wearing a long-sleeve t-shirt, sweatpants, and athletic shoes. He's got a ball cap on, and it's pulled down low. He must have known where the camera was because there's never a good view of his face."

"What's his hair like?"

"Brown, not long."

Addie slumped onto one of the dining chairs. "There's nothing distinguishing at all?"

"Oh, I didn't say that."

She straightened.

"His sweats are a little short for him, and they left a couple inches of ankle exposed," Bennett said. "There was a tattoo over his left outer ankle bone. I can't really make out what it is, though. A circular design of some sort."

"Can't you just enhance the picture?"

He gave a rueful chuckle. "It would take much more sophisticated software than I have. And even then, it might not be possible. The quality of the original footage isn't that great."

She scrunched her mouth to one side. Once again, it seemed a real-life investigation was messier and more difficult than TV shows had led her to believe.

"Any idea if he's connected with one of your other clients?" she asked.

"If I had to guess, I'd say it's unrelated to your aunt. I have a new case where the target roughly matches the description of the guy on the tape. He could have found out about it, maybe discovered the contract, and decided he didn't want to be the subject of a private investigation. Besides, the potential suspects we've been focused on for Kate's case are all women, and this guy seemed to be taking something very personally."

Well, Enzo was on the list in Chelsea's notebook, but Bennett's attacker definitely didn't match the build of Antonio's short, muscular nephew. Knowing the attack wasn't due to Kate's case was a slight weight off Addie's mind. She hated the idea that Bennett had been harmed because he was helping her.

"You're going to file a police report, right?" she asked.

"I am," he answered. "And before you ask, yes, I'm going to turn over the footage as well."

"Good," she said, genuinely relieved. "They haven't been very helpful with my aunt's case, but maybe it will be different with yours."

"We'll see." His tone didn't seem particularly hopeful.

"How are you feeling? Is the pain bad? Do you need anything?"

"Oh, I'll live," he said. "The headache is the worst of it, right now anyway. I just need to rest."

"Are you sure you're all right alone?" Addie's brow furrowed. "If you've got a concussion, it might not be safe for you to fall asleep with no one there to check on you."

"I asked the doc at the E.R., and she said it should be okay."

"Well, if you're sure."

"I really think some rest will do me good," he said. "But thank you for your concern, Addie."

"Of course. Don't hesitate to call me if you take a turn for the worse. I'll have my phone next to me all night."

"Thanks, but hopefully I won't need to do that," he said. "Say, have the police tried to follow up with you after Zelda's call?"

Her shoulders rounded forward. "Ugh. Yes. When Chelsea and I drove by earlier, McCann was looking in the window. She's definitely on the hunt."

"I suspect if you're too difficult to track down Zelda will just drop it," he said.

"I hope so. I'm not crazy about having to dodge the cops. I don't think I'm cut out for a life on the run."

He laughed, and it was a real one this time. Addie imagined his dimple making an appearance.

"Stay safe," he said.

"You too. Bye, Bennett."

Just as she ended the call, she got a text from Chelsea saying she was downstairs waiting to be let into Wild Rose. Addie ran down to unlock the door for her friend.

"Did you talk to Enzo?" Addie asked.

Chelsea nodded. "He helped Javier and Sofia Hernandez repaint their house last weekend, and they paid him a couple hundred dollars. That combined with what he made this week gave him enough for the ticket. He was really open about where all the funds came from. He seemed kind of proud and eager to talk about it, actually. I have no doubt he's telling the truth."

Addie wasn't sure if she was happy or sad to have eliminated Enzo as a suspect. It was good, she guessed, to have a definitive answer for once.

"Okay, well, at least we know," she said, letting out a breath. "I spoke to Bennett, and he said the guy who attacked him is most likely related to a different case he has."

"But he didn't know who it was?" Chelsea asked.

Addie shook her head.

"Well, it looks like we're officially down to Zelda and Lisette," Chelsea said. "If we're interpreting your tasseomancy vision correctly, it could still be either of them."

Addie was still leaning very much toward Zelda as the culprit, but Chelsea had clearly still not let go of Lisette as a possibility.

Chelsea placed a gentle hand on Addie's forearm. "You look exhausted, hon. Why don't you take it easy the rest of the evening? Tomorrow we can check on Bennett and see if we can make any progress with our last two suspects."

"That's probably a good idea," Addie admitted reluctantly.

After Chelsea left, Addie poured Lucky some more kibble, and he munched with enthusiasm. Feeling at loose ends, Addie moved around the apartment, straightening and tidying, while her thoughts bounced between Zelda, Lisette, and just how frustrating it was that the police had made no headway in finding Kate.

Well, maybe Addie shouldn't blame the entire department. It was Detective McCann who seemed to be the problem. Bennett had intimated the police, and McCann especially, weren't big fans of the secret society that Kate was supposedly aiding—the Shufflers. Did that mean the authorities actually knew Stargaze had a community of zombies in their midst? It seemed so.

And what would that mean for Aunt Kate if she was, in fact, one of them?

If.

Addie shook her head. How crazy was it that she was pinning her hopes on Kate being a *zombie*?

Lucky looked up from his bowl of food, his head swinging toward the stairs leading down to the store. He gave a little yip and then looked at Addie.

"What is it?" Addie asked. "Did you hear something?"

She went to the top of the stairs and listened. But Lucky didn't stop there. He trotted down and let out another excited little bark.

Oh no, was McCann back for another attempt at arresting Addie?

She knelt down and tried to peek at the front door. Someone was there, but it was too dark to say who.

"Helloooo?" called a muffled voice from outside. "Addie, is that you?"

That wasn't McCann, and whoever was out there had obviously spotted Addie. She reluctantly made her way down and flipped the switch that illuminated the lights along the storefront.

An older woman squinted at the sudden brightness, shielding her eyes. She looked vaguely familiar.

The woman waved as Addie approached. "Hello, dear, I need to speak with you," she called through the glass.

"How do you know my name?" Addie asked, hesitating.

"Oh, well, I'm Zelda's sister, Irene," she said. "I wanted to apologize for the unpleasantness my poor sister has dusted up and explain why she's been acting strangely."

Addie's brows shot up. The woman standing outside Wild Rose did indeed bear a resemblance to Zelda. In fact, Irene might have been the woman Addie had seen in the antique shop earlier whom she'd assumed was a customer.

She peered to the left, looking for Zelda.

"Don't worry, she's at home now," Irene said. "I just want to help clear the air."

Addie unlocked the door and held it open. She suddenly wished she'd stuck her pepper spray in her pocket, though at the same time felt a little ridiculous for thinking she'd need to defend herself against an old woman who seemed to mean no harm.

"As I mentioned, I'm Zelda's sister," Irene said. "She's been having some trouble, so I moved in with her a few days ago."

"What kind of trouble?" Addie asked, crossing her arms. She couldn't help flicking glances outside, half-expecting McCann to zoom up.

Lucky sat down between Addie and Irene, looking back and forth as if ready to take in the conversation.

Irene sighed and her expression turned from friendly to sad. "It's her mind. It's starting to go on her. It's reached a point where she might not be able to live on her own anymore."

Addie blinked, her brow wrinkling as she remembered Zelda's erratic behavior and her claim of bad days and memory problems.

"You mean dementia?" Addie asked quietly.

Irene nodded. "She's so stubborn, though, and doesn't want the help. It was a fight just to get her to agree to go to the doctor. She's gotten forgetful. She has angry outbursts sometimes."

Addie's gaze sharpened. "I'm very sorry to hear that, but there's something extremely important I need to ask you. Where was Zelda between eleven and midnight Thursday night?"

"Oh, she was at home asleep," Irene said, a quizzical look on her face.

"Were you there with her?"

"Yes, dear, I moved into her guest room on Tuesday."

"And were you awake during that time? Can you say for certain that Zelda didn't leave the house?" Addie pressed.

"I was awake. I'm a bit of a night owl, you see. I like to watch the late-night programs. That night, there was an actress I enjoy on the late, late one. Afterward, I was a bit peckish, so I made some soup. I didn't get to bed until one in the morning."

Addie's shoulders fell an inch or two. Zelda wasn't the culprit after all. But what about Kate's bag under the counter of the antique shop?

"I found my aunt's purse stuffed behind a trash can under the register in the antique shop," Addie said. "Can you explain how it got there?"

"Oh, my, yes. Kate came by Wednesday evening just before close and accidentally left it on the counter. I tried to bring it back here to her, but she didn't answer the door. I put her purse under the counter to make sure no one swiped it."

"I see," Addie said. "I'm sorry about Zelda's problems. It's kind of you to try to help her."

"Well, I need to apologize on her behalf for the trouble she's caused you," Irene said. "I didn't find out until it was too late that she called the police. But I spoke to them and then spoke to Zelda, and well . . ." She waved a hand through the air. "It's all been cleared up."

"So, she's not pressing charges against me? I'm not going to be arrested?"

"Oh, heavens, no," Irene said. "She feels bad about the whole thing."

Addie wasn't so sure of the part about Zelda feeling bad, but if the issue with the police had been dropped, that was good news.

"I appreciate you intervening," Addie said. "Did you know Zelda's been pressuring my aunt to sell her space?"

Irene gave a little shake of her head. "I'm still working on Zelda to drop that. There's no way she should be taking on more. If anything, we need to start scaling back the antique shop. Soon, it's going to be too much for her to handle. She doesn't want to hear it, but at some point, she's going to have to give it up."

A little stab of sadness pierced Addie's heart. Zelda had been a fixture on the corner of the block for as long as Addie could remember.

"I'm so sorry, that would really be the end of an era," Addie said.

Irene pressed her lips together and nodded. "I'll leave you be, now, dear."

After letting Irene out, Addie bolted the door. She shut off the lights and walked slowly through the dark store, mentally crossing Zelda off the list.

Was Lisette really the only suspect left?

Spotting the full trash bags from earlier, Addie found the door stop, propped the back door open, and lifted the bags. She hauled them over to the dumpster and set them down so she could open the lid. It took both hands and some heaving to swing the first bag up and over.

As she was reaching for the second bag, Lucky, who'd followed her out, started growling. Addie turned. Finding someone standing behind her, she let out a little startled shriek.

It was a man, and he had a baseball bat that was already in motion toward Addie's head.

On instinct, she dipped a shoulder and ducked. Missing his mark, the guy stumbled forward, the bat banging into the side of the dumpster.

Lucky was barking furiously and lunging in to bite at the backs of the man's legs.

"Help," Addie choked out. She tried again. "Help me!" Her scream ricocheted through the narrow alley.

The attacker turned to swing at Lucky, who darted out of the way.

Anger spiked through Addie. "Don't you dare hit my dog," she growled.

The man turned back at the sound of her voice, and she reached for the only object within arm's length. Grasping a rock the size of an egg, she chucked it. It hit him square in the nose. That was when she realized he had a bandana over his face, so only his eyes were visible.

He grabbed at his nose and swore. And that gave Addie a moment to really look at him. The bandana prevented her from making out his features, but he was wearing sweatpants, a long-sleeved t-shirt, and a ball cap. Just like Bennett's attacker.

Suddenly, a beam of light swung in from behind her. Then there was the unmistakable sound of a shotgun being cocked.

"Get down on the ground," a rich voice commanded.

It was Trey.

Addie peered around the dumpster to see him standing there gripping a flashlight against the barrel of a shotgun and sighting over it.

The attacker froze. Then he started backing up.

"Stop!" Trey ordered.

He bobbled the flashlight as he advanced, and the beam swept downward. It illuminated the attacker's ankle, giving Addie a clear view of the tattoo on the left ankle bone. It was a circular design—it looked like it might be a compass.

The attacker wheeled around and sprinted away.

Trey took off after him. Addie jumped to her feet and followed, Lucky bounding along at her left heel.

At the opening of the alley, she caught up with Trey.

He turned to Addie. "Are you okay? Do you need an ambulance?"

She dazedly shook her head. "I'm okay. He didn't hurt me."

"Here, hold this," he said and passed Addie the gun and flashlight. He pulled out his phone and dialed 911.

Chapter Nineteen

WHILE TREY MADE THE CALL to the police, Addie peered into the darkness. The attacker had gone off to the right, but he was an unusually fast runner and had quickly disappeared into the night.

After a quick conversation with the 911 dispatcher, Trey took the shotgun from Addie. "I don't think he'll try for round two, but the police will be here any second, so we'd better get back inside."

Addie's heart was still fluttering like a panicked bird. She shook her head, trying to catch her breath as she walked with Trey back to the rear door of Wild Rose.

"If you wouldn't have shown up . . ." She couldn't finish the sentence.

He gave her a little smile. "You were holding your own. More rocks, and you would have taken him down. You've got good aim."

She managed a faint smile back, but she was feeling a little lightheaded.

Inside, Trey propped the shotgun behind the checkout counter and found the lights. A moment later, a police cruiser pulled up outside.

It was Officer Davis.

He took her statement about the attack, told her another officer would be posted outside the rest of the night, and left. No Detective McCann, which was a huge relief.

Addie sat heavily at one of the café tables.

"Hey, do you want to call Chelsea?" Trey asked.

She shook her head. "I don't want to wake her. I'm safe here in the shop, and there will be an officer patrolling outside."

"I could leave the gun, if you'd like. You don't have to keep it loaded."

"Oh, that's okay," she said. "Truly, I'll be fine. I do need to make a call about the attack, though."

She wasn't trying to kick him out—on the contrary, she appreciated having him there—but she really needed to talk to Bennett. The same man had attacked him. Or tried, anyway. It had to be connected to Kate's case.

And that meant Addie had been on the wrong track. The suspect list was all wrong.

"Sure," Trey said. "You've got my number if you need anything."

She nodded and walked him to the door. "Thank you again. You saved me. That was no flat tire by the side of the road. That was real. Way too real. I don't know how I can ever repay you."

"No need for repayment," he said. "I'm happy to do it."

On impulse, she threw her arms around his neck. He gave a little grunt of surprise but squeezed her back.

"Thank you again." She pulled away and stood there feeling a little awkward. "I know I keep saying that, but I don't think I can say it enough."

After Trey left, Addie went upstairs and sat in the dark, feeling more hopeless than she'd felt since she'd arrived in Stargaze.

She'd been so sure she and Chelsea had the right list of people, so confident that one of the suspects on the list was responsible for hurting Aunt Kate.

But Addie was wrong.

The only suspect remaining in Chelsea's notebook was Lisette, and Addie was sure the volatile café owner had nothing to do with Kate's attack.

No, the man who'd tried to smash in Addie's head, who'd beat up Bennett, that was the one they should have been looking for all along.

Problem was, she had nothing to go on except that tattoo.

And that man was out there somewhere.

The thought left Addie cold.

She picked up her phone and dialed Bennett.

He answered on the third ring.

"Addie, is something wrong?"

"Yes," she said heavily. "We were on the wrong track."

She described the attack in the alley.

"It was definitely the same guy who jumped you," she said.

Bennett cursed under his breath. "Are you sure you're okay? I can come over there. The meds have worn off, and I'm fine to drive now."

"No, no," she said. "I wasn't trying to make you feel badly. I'm fine, really. Just a little shaken. Honestly, I think I'm less upset about what happened than I am about feeling so blindsided. Figuratively, I mean. Blindsided in terms of focusing on the wrong people."

A lump started to form in her throat, and she had to stop talking for a second.

"Now, I feel like I have nothing to go on," she said, her voice wavering. "I don't know who that man is or why he would have attacked Kate."

"Well, we're going to figure that out," Bennett said, his voice firm and determined. "I promise."

"Okay," she said. "I'll talk to you tomorrow."

He seemed hesitant to say goodbye, but Addie wasn't in the mood to chat any further. She ended the call and set down her phone. Lucky jumped up beside her, and she hugged him into her side.

"You saved me too, you know," she said and then kissed the top of his head. "Thank you for being so fierce."

He licked her cheek and then lay down with his head on her thigh.

Addie sat there in the dark for another hour before she finally dozed off.

⸺⸻❦⸻⸺

THE NEXT MORNING, ADDIE CALLED Chelsea to let her know about the attack and the disappointing discovery that they'd been wrong about the suspects.

"You were right about Zelda," Addie said. "You never thought she was the culprit, and you picked up on something about her that was off." She went on to recount the conversation with Irene.

"Dementia," Chelsea said quietly. "Her aura was showing something I didn't quite understand at the time. But that must be what it was. Poor Zelda. And poor you, Addie. Geez, what a night you had."

They commiserated for a few minutes, and Chelsea promised to connect later in the day.

No longer fearful about Zelda or Detective McCann, Addie decided to treat herself to a latte and scone from La Petite Patisserie and get something for Bennett. Maybe the decision to go to the café also had something to do with demonstrating she had no intention of letting Lisette bully her.

Addie walked down to the bookstore and crossed Pine Avenue with Lucky trotting at her side. Renaldo and Octavia were just opening up Hair Affair. When Addie waved to them, Octavia waved back but Renaldo quickly ducked his head and turned away.

At the café, Addie tied Lucky's leash to a table outside, squared her shoulders, and strode in.

Lisette glared but didn't say anything.

"I'll have a vanilla latte, two peach scones, and whatever drink Bennett Brooks usually orders," Addie said.

She paid, feeling satisfied about not letting Lisette push her around, and moved to the side to wait for her order. She pulled out her phone and sent Bennett a quick text letting him know she'd be arriving with coffee in fifteen minutes.

After picking up the paper bag with the scones and a cardboard drink holder with two to-go cups, she collected Lucky, crossed the street, and walked past Grinning Catfish Brewery to her car. With the dog in the back and the food in the front, she pulled away and headed to Bennett's house.

When she got there, she found him sitting in one of the two chairs on his front porch. She'd hoped for a peek inside his house, but it appeared she wasn't going to get it. He stood and came to help her with the drinks.

"How are you feeling today?" she asked.

"Sore, but I'll live," he said. "How about you? You sounded really discouraged last night."

"I was. I am."

He waited for her to sit before lowering himself to his own chair, Addie noted with appreciation. Nice manners never went out of style.

Feeling forlorn, she sipped her latte. "I don't know who this guy is or how to track him down, and I still have no idea if Aunt Kate is okay. Alive or, you know, alive-ish."

Bennett shook his head. "I'm sorry, Addie. For what it's worth, I was blindsided, too."

"What *is* this guy's connection to everything?" Addie mused aloud. "He really seemed to believe that you and I were investigating him. He must have thought we were closing in on proving he was the one who attacked Aunt Kate. And yet, we had no idea he was involved."

"It's a head scratcher," he said with a sigh.

They sipped in silence for a moment, and Addie tried to muster up some hope. She reached for the bag, passed Bennett a scone, and then took a bite of her own. It nearly melted in her mouth. The bread was the perfect balance between moist and crumbly, and the pieces of peach were like little morsels of summer on her tongue.

She swallowed and glanced at Bennett. "Your job must be hard."

"What makes you say that?"

"Well, TV and movies make detective work look so much more straightforward. There's always a clear logic that leads you from A to B to C. It's tidy. This . . ." She shook her head. "This has been so messy. Unclear. Difficult."

"*People* are messy and difficult," he said with a sympathetic chuckle. "But that's what makes them interesting. It makes being a P.I. interesting, too. TV shows follow a formula. Real life isn't so obedient. As you said, people actually aren't that rational. We like to think we are, but we're really emotional beings."

"Yeah, I guess so," she said faintly.

She couldn't help thinking of Jeremy, and how she never would have guessed he was unhappy enough to cheat on her. For all she believed, they were like any other couple with ups and downs and little arguments that never quite got resolved. She'd thought they were good together. They'd ticked all the right boxes. But maybe that was just on paper. Maybe that was just her trying to break the relationship down into a formula. Trying to apply too much logic.

She finished her scone and brushed crumbs from her fingers as an idea began to form in her mind.

"I'm going to head back home," she said, rising. "There's something I need to do. I don't know if it'll help, but I need to try."

He looked up in surprise. "Okay. I'm going to see what I can do with that footage. If you remember anything else about the guy who came after you in the alley, be sure and let me know."

"Will do," she said.

"And thanks for the breakfast. It was nice to have some company."

She gave him a little smile. "You're welcome. Glad to do it."

Back at Wild Rose Teas and Apothecary, Addie lowered the shades in the front windows. Then she started some hot water in the electric kettle and got the dolphin cup and saucer. This time, she chose her favorite jasmine green tea, placing two generous pinches of leaves into the cup.

Lucky settled down on a folded blanket Addie had placed on the floor as a dog bed and watched her move around the shop.

"Yes, I'm going to try to read the tea leaves," she said. "I know it seems crazy, and I don't really want to do it, but right now I'll take anything that might help us catch that man. I can't go into zombieland to find Aunt Kate, so the least I can do is make sure the person who hurt her pays for it."

Lucky thumped his tail in a seemingly encouraging gesture.

The button on the kettle popped. She poured steaming water over the leaves and then took the cup and saucer to the same table where she'd sat before.

Sipping slowly from the cup, she focused on her desire to identify and find the man who'd attacked her and Bennett and most likely also Kate. It was an effort, though, because her mind kept skipping around, refusing to settle on that one thought. With an exasperated sigh, she leaned forward and braced her elbows on the table, squinted, and tried harder.

But halfway through the tea, she realized it wasn't working.

She grumbled under her breath and pushed back in disgust. She paced for a moment and then walked over to the shelves and let her gaze scan across the bottles. Without really thinking, she reached for a large jar labeled "Infinity Tea." She didn't remember it, but when she opened the jar and inhaled the aroma of the herbs inside, she knew it immediately. This had to be one of Kate's favorites because the smell took Addie back to summer days hanging out in the shop with her aunt.

Choosing a different cup and saucer, this one plain white, Addie prepared some Infinity Tea.

Standing at the counter where Kate had spent so many hours helping clients, Addie sipped and thought about her aunt and how good she was, how much she, of all people, deserved justice.

Before Addie knew it, she was down to the dregs at the bottom. She swirled the cup, flipped it over on the saucer, and then turned it right-side up.

The electric flutters took over her body, speeding through her as if they'd been waiting to be released. Addie swayed a little and then leaned into the counter to keep her balance.

She peered into the cup, expecting to see little images in the tea globs, but there was only one. It was an arrow pointing away from her.

And then the whispers came.

"*Look up, look up, look up.*"

Look up? Addie tilted her head back to glance at the ceiling, wondering if she was supposed to be seeing something else. But there was nothing out of the ordinary up there.

She tilted her gaze toward the door, which didn't have blinds, just as someone walked past. It was Renaldo Hernandez.

She set the cup and saucer down, and the sensations faded.

Were the leaves trying to tell her something about Renaldo, or had she missed the message entirely?

Was her supposed "gift" sending her straight to the culprit? Could Renaldo be the attacker?

"Only one way to find out," she said, hurrying toward the door to catch him.

Chapter Twenty

ADDIE HURRIED OUT TO THE sidewalk, her pulse bumping as she caught sight of Renaldo disappearing around the corner of Zelda's A to Z Antiques.

Breaking into a jog, she went after him.

"Renaldo," she called when she spotted him.

He looked back, but instead of stopping, he sped up.

Addie frowned. Was he seriously trying to avoid her? What was up with that?

She pumped her elbows harder, and when she got around the next corner, he wasn't there. But the door to Javier's was drifting closed. He must have gone into his parents' restaurant.

She yanked the door open and went into the establishment, which was relatively dark compared to the bright sunshine outside. Blinking and squinting, she peered around. A woman who looked like Octavia but about twenty-five years older was wrapping silverware in white paper napkins. She spotted Addie and walked over.

"We're not open for lunch yet," the woman said with a polite smile. "Not for another hour."

"Oh, I'm not here for lunch, though your chicken mole tacos are my all-time favorite," Addie said. "Did Renaldo come in here?"

The woman looked around, perplexed. "I haven't seen him."

Addie shoved her hair behind her ears. "Darn it, I thought I saw him."

She was just about to turn to leave when a face peeked through the window between the kitchen and dining room. It was him.

"There he is," Addie said.

The woman turned and said something to Renaldo in Spanish. He didn't respond. She spoke again, and he grimaced and then with obvious reluctance moved toward the door leading into the dining room and joined Addie and the woman, who had to be Sofia, his mother.

"This nice young lady is here to speak with you, Naldo," Sofia said, seeming to load the words with significance.

Sofia returned to the silverware, and Addie leaned closer to Renaldo to whisper, "Were you really trying to run away from me?"

He cast a furtive look back at his mother and then pointed to the door. "Let's talk somewhere else."

"Hey—" Addie warned, thinking he might use the opportunity to run again.

"I'm not going to bolt. Don't worry," he said, his tone resigned. He pointed down the block at a parking lot across the street. "There's a fountain with a couple of benches down there."

They walked quickly past Slice of Pie and another eatery called FYSH that Addie hadn't noticed before. Then they crossed Main to the parking lot. Renaldo seemed to relax a little once they were well away from Javier's Mexican Restaurant.

When they sat down on the bench, Addie angled toward him and for the first time realized there was bruising around one of his eyes.

"Oh my gosh, is that a black eye?" she exclaimed. "What happened?"

He brushed his fingers over his brow. "I'd rather not talk about it, if you don't mind."

"Okay," she said, her brow knitting in concern. "Look, I just wanted to ask you a couple of questions, but honestly, the way you were acting back there has me rethinking what I should be asking you."

"Why's that?" he asked with trepidation.

"Well, it's pretty suspicious that you see me and then take off," she said.

"Sorry, I just thought you might have seen—actually, never mind." He'd crossed his arms tightly over his chest.

He was muscular, but he was a bit too short to be the man who'd tried to brain her with a bat in the alley, so at least she didn't have to ask him if he'd attacked anyone recently.

"What do you want to ask me?" he prompted, after she hesitated for a second or two too long.

"You know, I thought I knew, but now I'm a little confused," she said, her mind whirling. She couldn't very well tell him that tea leaves and voices in her head had told her to follow him. "I guess—I guess it would be this: there were some attacks recently. First my Aunt Kate. Then a man was attacked a block away from the tea shop, and last night the same guy tried to come after me."

Renaldo's dark eyes widened. "Oh no, that's terrible. Did you get hurt?"

She shook her head. "This probably seems like it's coming out of the blue, but do you know anyone who might have done that? A tallish man, strong, and well, angry? He came after me with a bat.

The only thing that saved me was my neighbor, Trey, who came out with a gun. Trey and my dog Lucky, that is."

Renaldo's gaze had drifted down to a spot on the pavement in front of them, and he didn't say anything right away.

"These two incidents, the one with the man a block away and with you in the alley, they happened last night?" he asked quietly.

Her breath caught. He seemed on the verge of telling her something important.

"Yes," she said.

"What I'm about to tell you could cause a lot of trouble for me," he said, his eyes still lowered. "But I can't stay quiet about something like this."

She waited, holding her breath.

"Someone asked me—no, *threatened* me—late last night," he said. "This person told me I'd have to vouch for him if someone came asking."

"Vouch for him?" Addie repeated, her brow creasing in confusion. "What do you mean by that?"

"He was asking me to provide a false alibi, I think."

Addie's mouth dropped open. "Who was it?"

"Lance. That rager jerk who owns Ripped."

The world seemed to tilt sideways.

L for Lance.

The vision of the lightning bolt between the two people—was that something significant that had happened between Kate and Lance? The violence of his attack, maybe?

"Renaldo, did he give you that black eye?" she whispered.

He gave a tiny nod.

"I don't understand, though," she said. "Why would he target you to be his false alibi?"

"Because he knows a secret about me," Renaldo said, his expression turning to one of misery.

Addie blinked, and then her eyes widened as she recalled what she'd seen passing between the bookstore man and Renaldo. The smiles they'd traded. Renaldo's wink.

"Does it have something to do with the tall man at Enchanted Pages?" she asked.

"Yes," he said, his voice barely audible.

"Oh," she said, drawing the word out on a long breath. "For what it's worth, I won't tell anyone."

"I appreciate that," he said. "But if I get mixed up in all of this, it's bound to come out."

"But you need to report what he did to you, Renaldo," Addie said, peering at his black eye with distress.

"I don't want the details of my personal life splashed all over the place," he said.

"Your family doesn't know, I take it?"

He shook his head.

She pressed her lips together for a long moment. "Well, I for one don't think you should have to hide your happiness. That's not right."

"You probably don't come from a family like mine," he said with a small sigh.

"You're right. I don't. But I bet your parents want you to be happy."

"Yeah." He didn't sound like he really believed it.

"Thank you for telling me, Renaldo," she said. "Lance needs to be punished for what he's done to you as well as to Kate, Bennett, and me. I hope it doesn't end up costing you your privacy, but I want you to know that I'll never forget what you've done. I know we don't really know each other, but if you ever need anything, I'm your girl."

He smiled faintly. "Thanks. I should probably get back to the restaurant. I'm supposed to be helping my parents with some accounting."

She nodded, and they both stood.

"Have you seen Lance today, by chance?" she asked, realizing she hadn't noticed whether Ripped was open.

Renaldo shook his head. "No, but if you want to find him, I'd ask Georgia." He pulled out his phone. "I have her number from back when they first moved into the space next to Hair Affair."

He gave Addie the phone number.

"Thanks," she said.

They parted ways, Renaldo heading back to Javier's and Addie to Wild Rose Teas and Apothecary.

She walked in a daze, her head swimming. Lance's build and stature matched the attacker's. He had to be the one responsible for all three—no, four—attacks. But why had he hurt Aunt Kate in the first place?

It probably had to do with the trouble between him and Georgia.

Addie's sneaker's scuffed to a halt. The lightning bolt was between Georgia and Lance, symbolizing the rupture in the relationship.

Renaldo was right. Addie needed to find Georgia.

Lifting her phone, Addie quickly found Bennett's name and hit the call button.

"It was Lance, the guy who owns the supplement store across from Wild Rose," she said without preamble, her words tumbling out in a rush.

"How do you know?" Bennett asked.

She quickly described her conversation with Renaldo. "I don't know what to do next, though."

Her fingers trembled slightly as she unlocked the tea shop.

"We need proof," he said. "Or at least something really convincing linking him to the attacks."

"I don't think I have anything strong enough. I need to talk to Georgia. I bet she can provide proof."

"Try calling her and let me know how it goes," Bennett said. "If she doesn't respond, be sure and call me back."

"Will you pinpoint her whereabouts using her phone number?" Addie asked hopefully.

"Now you're thinking like a P.I." She could hear the faint grin in his voice. "Text me her number, and I'll get on it."

"We're so close, Bennett," she said. "I just don't want to mess this up."

"We're not going to mess it up. He's not going to get away with what he did."

"Do you think Lance knows where Kate is?" she asked.

"I doubt it, honestly," Bennett said.

She didn't think so, either. As she'd begun to suspect earlier, it was seeming more and more as if the attack and the disappearance were two different mysteries.

They both hung up, and Addie paused for a moment, silently rehearsing what she'd say to Georgia and then called her.

Six rings and then a voicemail greeting. Addie's hopes faltered as she left a message that she hoped sounded urgent enough to get Georgia to respond ASAP but didn't alarm her. Then Addie sent a text identifying herself and essentially repeating the voice message she'd left. But after she hit send, she froze. What if Lance had access to Georgia's phone? Had Addie given away too much?

Too late to take it back.

She let Bennett know that Georgia wasn't picking up, and he responded that he'd try tracking her location.

Addie went to the window and peered across the street at Ripped. The store was dark, the closed sign still visible. She huffed an impatient sigh. How could she track down Lance?

She snapped her fingers. "Enzo."

Once again stepping outside and locking up the tea shop, she retraced her earlier route around the block, ending up at Slice of Pie.

Antonio was at the counter taking early lunch orders, and Addie spotted Enzo in the back by the ovens. She moved to the side and tried to catch his eye. When he looked up, she smiled and waved. He grinned broadly and swaggered to the front, wiping his hands on the apron tied around his waist.

"Where's Blondie?" he asked. "I thought the two of us kinda hit it off."

"Oh, uh, she's working," Addie said. "But hey, how well do you know that guy Lance who runs Ripped?"

He raised a shoulder and let it drop. "We talk about lifting and nutrition and that sort of thing, but it's not like we socialize and whatnot."

"So you don't know where he'd hang out when he's not at the store?"

"Home, I guess? Maybe the gym?" Enzo tapped his chin. "He mentioned a camper. He told me him and his girl take it down to Jade Lake or go up in the mountains sometimes. He could be camping."

Addie perked up. If Lance were paranoid about getting caught, and the closure of Ripped did seem to indicate he might be in hiding, he wouldn't be at his usual haunts. But the camper gave him the option of being mobile.

"Do you have his phone number, by chance?" Addie asked.

"Nah, sorry." Antonio called to Enzo, and he turned. "I better get back there before Uncle Tony kicks my butt."

"Right, I'm sorry I interrupted your shift. Thanks for your help."

"No problem. Tell Blondie hello."

Addie forced a smile. "Her name is *Chelsea*. Not Blondie. Use her name, okay?"

She turned and left, her smile dropping and her eyes rolling upward as she pushed the door. Chelsea's sweetness didn't mean she deserved to be treated disrespectfully.

On the way back to Wild Rose, Addie texted Bennett to let him know she didn't have Lance's number yet, but she was trying.

Then she called Chelsea and told her the short version of what had happened that morning.

When Addie said Lance's name, Chelsea gasped.

"You did it," she said. "You figured out who it was."

"Yeah, but I still need to find him," Addie said. "And more than that, I need solid evidence. I wish Georgia would answer her phone. I'm pretty sure she could fill in enough gaps for us to go to the police. Plus, if she's with Lance, I'm worried for her. It's pretty obvious he's dangerous. What if he knows about her affair with the lawyer?"

"Well, I happen to know a lot of the good camping spots around Stargaze," Chelsea said. "Let me grab my purse, and I'll come and get you. We can take a little tour of the area."

"Great idea. Let's figure out their location and then work on getting Georgia away from him."

Chapter Twenty-One

ADDIE DECIDED SHE AND CHELSEA should take the Ford Escape instead of the little yellow bug, in case they ended up on dirt roads.

Addie put her phone on speaker and called Bennett and let him know what they were doing.

"I don't suppose you've got a location for Georgia's phone that's, oh, I don't know, right next to Jade Lake?" she asked hopefully.

"Last location I could pull up was on the highway, looks like," he said. He gave the coordinates, and Chelsea punched them into her GPS. "But that was late last night. I'm guessing her phone's been turned off since then. I'm working on getting Lance's cell number."

By the way he said "working," Addie wondered if some hacking was involved. Not that she had any objection. Lance had lost his right to any courtesy or privacy when he'd attacked four people.

"That location is a starting point, anyway," Addie said. "We'll go there and see what's nearby."

"Wait, Addie?" Bennet said. "I know you're eager to find Lance, but you have to promise me you won't approach or confront him. I wouldn't even do that."

"We won't," Addie said. "I want to figure out where he is and make sure he doesn't slip away. But if there's an opportunity to get to Georgia, I'm going to take it. If he knows about the affair, he may be holding her against her will. Or worse."

Addie could almost hear Bennett's urge to argue with her in the short silence that followed.

"He's dangerous. Obviously," Bennett said. "I understand your intentions, but you don't know if he has guns or what."

"I swear I won't do anything rash."

"Okay. I'm going to keep working on getting Lance's cell and keep pinging Georgia's number and hope we get an updated location."

Chelsea gave her directions to the coordinates, which took them around Jade Lake and up the highway that followed the river that fed the lake.

"Are there more campgrounds up this way?" Addie asked, not remembering the area well.

"There's one, but it's large and well-known, and I don't think that's where we'll find them," Chelsea said. "There are other turn-offs that mostly only locals know about."

"Has Lance been here long enough to be considered a local?"

Chelsea snorted. "Not by a long shot. It's only been a year or so since Ripped opened. But somebody might have blabbed. Or if he and Georgia went exploring a lot, they might have found some of the good spots on their own." She pointed up ahead to the right. "Take that turn. There's a clearing about a half mile in."

"What if they hear us coming?" Addie asked.

She hadn't thought about how noisy their approach might be.

"Um, how good are you in reverse?" Chelsea asked.

"I guess we'll find out."

It turned out there was no need for worry because the clearing was empty. But when Addie spotted a ring of rocks with charred wood still in it, she put the car in park and jumped out to inspect it.

Sure enough, there was some partially burned trash in the ring. Chelsea joined her.

"Look," Addie pointed. "That's a protein-bar wrapper." She bent and picked it up. There was a price sticker on the back. "The tag says Ripped, and there's still some heat coming off the rocks."

"They were here recently, then." Chelsea turned a full circle, looking around.

"I bet they just took off this morning," Addie said. "We're on the right track, but the question is, are they going to hang around the area or take off?"

Chelsea shook her head. "No idea."

"I think if they were going to hightail it out, they wouldn't have bothered camping here last night," Addie said. "They may try to come back to the store before they go. Grab cash, inventory, whatever."

"Hm, that's a good thought. Do you want to keep looking for them or stake out the store?" Chelsea asked.

"If they clean out Ripped, it'll probably be in the middle of the night. We should try to get to Georgia before then."

"Here, I'll drive," Chelsea said. "Maybe I'll get some intuitive signs about where they are. You should try to get an update from Bennett."

Addie dialed Bennett and let him know what she'd found at the clearing.

"That's good news," Bennett said.

"Any luck with the cell signals?" she asked.

"No, but I'm starting to think maybe they're in an area where there's no cell service."

"Oh, huh. That's unfortunate."

"Well, they're probably going to want to connect at some point," he said. "People hate to be out of contact for too long."

"True. Let me know if anything pops up."

"I will," he said. "But your promise still stands. Don't tangle with Lance."

"Promise," she said and then ended the call and turned to Chelsea. "He thinks they're in an area with no service."

"Hey, there's a road that goes up a ravine off the river," Chelsea said. "The hillsides there are so steep phones don't work."

"How far is it from here?"

"Two or three miles."

"Space enough to camp?"

Chelsea gave her a quick grin. "Yup."

"That sounds very promising," Addie said.

They'd reached the main highway, and Chelsea took a left. While she drove, Addie did some poking around online. It didn't take long to find some social media pages for Ripped. Lance was tagged in some of the photos, which led her to his profile, where most of the pics were public.

Addie scrolled through them. Her fingers went still when she got to one of Lance and Georgia posing in front of an RV towed by a large truck with expensive-looking shiny rims.

"Hey," she said. "I found a photo of their RV. It's gray and white and it's connected to a big black pickup."

Chelsea sucked in a sharp breath. "Like the one headed right toward us?"

Addie swung her gaze up in time to see a black truck approaching from the opposite direction.

"Get down," Chelsea said urgently.

Addie ducked. "Is it him?" she hissed and watched Chelsea turn her head as the truck went past.

"Yeah, that was him. No RV. Also, no Georgia."

Addie sat up. "He must have disconnected the truck from the RV. If she's not with him, she's got to be in it."

"All alone." Chelsea sped up.

"This is our chance," Addie said, her pulse spiking with adrenaline.

"But do you think we should follow Lance?" Chelsea said. "What if he's leaving? Like, *leaving* leaving?"

"Shoot, you think he'd really take off without Georgia?"

"I dunno. But he could be going back to Stargaze."

Addie blasted out a breath. What to do?

"You know what? I saw his tattoo. I can identify him as my attacker, and with the tape we can prove he's the one who jumped Bennett. If we can get Lance arrested, then there'll be time to tie him to Kate's attack. I don't want him getting away. Let's go after him."

Chelsea pulled over, swung a quick U-turn, and then jammed on the gas.

Addie called Bennett. "Lance is headed toward Stargaze, and we're going after him. I know we wanted definitive proof to tie him to all three attacks, but we can at least tie him to mine and yours."

"Okay, I'll call the cops right now," Bennett said.

Addie gave him the description of the truck and hung up.

"Do you really think Lance would be dumb enough to go to Ripped right now?" Addie asked.

"I'm not sure," Chelsea said. She'd shifted forward, her eyes glued to the road in the distance. "Maybe he's running home."

Addie anxiously peered through the windshield. The highway wound back and forth a bit through a canyon, so she couldn't see very far ahead.

Chelsea let out a little squeak. "There's the truck!"

Addie flapped her hand. "Ease off the gas a little. We don't want to seem like we're following him."

Staying about a half mile behind Lance, Addie held her breath every time the truck disappeared around a curve and then let it out in a sigh of relief each time the black vehicle came back into view.

Addie couldn't help going over and over in her mind what'd happened to Aunt Kate, trying to understand the incident knowing Lance was the attacker.

What was his motive?

"I still don't understand why Lance did what he did to Kate," Addie said. "I mean, it seems like it's got to be something related to Georgia."

"How do you know that?"

"The thing in the tea leaves," Addie said. "The two people and the lightning bolt. I'm pretty sure that's Georgia and Lance."

Chelsea's eyes widened. "Yeah, that makes sense. An affair is a pretty catastrophic thing to happen in a relationship."

"Right, but there's got to be something else, too." Addie frowned, concentrating. "I just don't know hardly anything about Lance."

"He likes obnoxiously loud music. Has a violent temper and a baseball bat. Works out. Eats protein bars in the woods. Has a girlfriend who's cheating on him and pregnant with another man's child."

"That last one's got to be the key," Addie said with a dry, humorless laugh.

"Well, we know Georgia went to Kate for help."

"Yeah, she wanted Kate to help her end the pregnancy that resulted from the affair."

"Do you think Lance knew Georgia went to Kate?" Chelsea asked.

"I'm not sure. But maybe. Kate must have done something that really pissed him off. Would he really be that mad about the herbs, though? Kate didn't even end up giving them to Georgia."

Chelsea shrugged. "If he didn't know Georgia had an affair yet, but found out she was pregnant, maybe he was really excited about being a dad? And was angry at Kate if he thought she was taking that away from him?"

"Eh, I don't know about that. Something just doesn't line up."

"Yeah, I agree," Chelsea said.

Addie watched the truck ahead. "Think he knows he's being followed?"

"No. I think he's got something more important on his mind." Chelsea's brow furrowed. "It's got to be important if he's taking the risk of going back to Stargaze, right?"

"True."

Addie's phone jangled.

"Hi, Bennett," she said. "What did the police say?"

"They're sending a car your way. It's going to pass you going the opposite direction and then circle back to follow at a distance," he said. "Another car will be waiting on the south edge of Stargaze. They don't want to risk a chase out there on a curvy mountain road, so they'd rather stop him at the edge of town."

"What should we do?" Addie asked.

"Try to stay on him, and if he does anything other than keep driving to Stargaze, call the number I'm about to text you. It's a direct line to McCann's cell."

She straightened, suddenly feeling like she had a real role in making sure Lance was apprehended. "Got it."

"We just need to keep doing what we're doing," Addie said to Chelsea. "A cruiser is going to pass us and come back around to follow."

Chelsea tightened her grip on the steering wheel.

"Are you okay to drive?" Addie asked.

"Oh, I'm great," she said. "I was just imagining Lance in handcuffs. We can't let him get away."

They were passing Jade Lake, which meant the south edge of Stargaze was near.

Chelsea shortened the distance between the Escape and the black truck.

"There's the other cruiser," Addie said, pointing up ahead.

The cop waited for Lance to pass and then pulled out in front of the Escape. Addie held her breath as she watched the cruiser follow the truck.

Lance made a couple of turns.

"Where do you think he's going?" Addie asked.

Chelsea squinted. "Hmm, not sure. Home, maybe? I think he lives in southeast Stargaze."

"Why isn't he getting pulled over?" Addie muttered anxiously.

"Oh, wait, I know where he's headed," Chelsea said.

Addie lifted her phone. "Where?"

"The bank."

Punching the number Bennett had sent and then putting the phone to her ear, Addie called Detective McCann and told her where the truck was likely going.

"Great, I'll send another car to cut him off," McCann said quickly and then hung up.

"They're going to sandwich him," Addie said, her pulse starting to race with anticipation.

"I bet he's going to empty his account," Chelsea said.

Addie sent a quick update to Bennett and then shoved her phone in the pocket of her sweatshirt.

Lance turned into the bank parking lot. The cruiser followed.

"Pull over there, Chels," Addie said, pointing to the curb, her pulse thumping.

Chelsea steered off the road. "Wait, you're not going to—"

But Addie was already jumping out.

Two more cruisers sped up and then screeched to a stop. The cops had Lance penned into the parking lot. The officers jumped out and drew their guns, all of them pointing at the truck. McCann's sedan screeched to a stop, and she popped out and joined them.

Addie ran across the street, her heart in her throat. All she could think about was making sure Lance didn't get away. She would tackle him to the ground herself, if she had to.

One of the officers was on a bullhorn, commanding Lance to come out with his hands up.

Addie stopped at the back of McCann's car, her pulse pounding and her breath coming fast.

The truck door swung open, and Lance climbed down with his arms raised.

Two of the officers ran forward and forced him to the ground.

Addie raced across the lot.

"Hey!" Detective McCann hollered. "Stop, Addie!"

But Addie ignored the shouts. All she could think about was making sure Lance went to jail long enough for her to prove he'd also attacked Kate.

The officers had closed in, some of them helping to cuff Lance and others searching the truck.

Addie got to Lance just as two officers hauled him to his feet. They were reciting his rights.

She crouched next to Lance's left foot and yanked down his sock. There was the compass tattoo on his ankle.

McCann was pulling at Addie's shoulder, but she jerked out of the detective's grip.

"This is the man who attacked me. I saw this tattoo," Addie said, standing up and pointing at Lance's ankle. She turned to him, her hands balling into fists. "You attacked my aunt, too! Where is she?"

"Addie, let them do their job," McCann was saying, again trying to pull Addie away.

But Addie trailed along behind as Lance was walked over to one of the cruisers.

"Where is Kate?" she yelled at Lance.

He wouldn't even look at her. In the back seat of the cruiser, he stared straight ahead. One of the officers slammed the door, and Addie beat on the window with her palm.

"Where is she?" she hollered again.

"Addie," said a familiar voice behind her.

She turned to find Bennett there.

"Hey," he said gently. "You did it. He's going to jail."

"I know," she said. "But I still don't know where Kate is."

"I don't think Lance knows where she is, either," Bennett said.

She'd already known it, known that Lance wasn't the one who'd taken Kate away. But part of her had still hoped.

Chapter Twenty-Two

BENNETT WAS TRYING TO COMFORT Addie, but she ran a hand over her hair and looked around, distraught.

"We have to go get Georgia," she said. "I think Lance left her somewhere in the woods."

Chelsea had joined them, and McCann was headed their way after talking to the officers who were hauling Lance into the station.

The detective did not look pleased.

"You could have been shot, running into the middle of an apprehension that way," she said to Addie.

"They already had him on the ground," Addie said, not in the mood for McCann's lecture. "Besides, that's not important right now. We've got to find Lance's girlfriend. She could be hurt."

"I think I know where she is," Chelsea said.

"I'll drive," Bennett offered.

"No," McCann said. "We'll send officers to get her."

Addie shook her head. "I want to speak to her. Sorry, but you're not going to stop me. We know where Georgia is. You don't. So, we're going whether you like it or not."

Addie got into the front seat of Bennett's Jeep, and Chelsea climbed into the back. A cruiser followed them as they drove out of town. Chelsea gave directions, and they ended up at a small campground in the trees.

"That's the RV," Addie said, recognizing the vehicle from the photo she'd found on Lance's page.

The door of the RV opened, and Georgia appeared.

"Oh, thank goodness," Addie said.

Bennett stopped, and she hopped out.

"Are you okay?" she called to Georgia.

The woman peered at her in confusion. "Addie?"

"Lance has been arrested," Addie said. "He attacked Bennett and tried to do the same to me. He also seriously injured my aunt."

Georgia's face paled. "Oh my god."

"You didn't know?" Addie asked.

She shook her head. "I knew she was missing, but I—well, I didn't know Lance was involved, but I'd started to wonder."

The police cruiser eased to a stop behind Bennett's Jeep, and Officer Davis stepped out.

"You need to come with us, ma'am," he called to Georgia.

She looked at him, dazed. "Okay, let me just get my purse."

"Wait!" Officer Davis said. "Stay right there. I'll accompany you into the RV."

Georgia nodded.

"I don't think she was involved," Addie said quietly to Bennett and Chelsea.

"I think you're right," Bennett said.

When Georgia turned around to go into the RV, something clicked in Addie's mind. She inhaled sharply.

"Lance didn't mean to hurt Kate," she said. "The attack was meant for Georgia."

"How do you know?" Chelsea asked.

"Because Georgia looks exactly like Kate from the back. I noticed it a couple of days ago. I saw Georgia looking in the window of Wild Rose and for a split second thought she was my aunt. They have the same build and the same hair. They even dress similarly."

The three of them watched Georgia and Officer Davis emerge from the RV.

"Lance must have learned that Georgia had an affair. He knew she and Kate were friends. I bet when Lance realized his mistake, he took the cash from the register to try to make it look like a robbery," Addie said.

Georgia had stopped nearby, listening.

"But why would Lance have thought Georgia was alone in Wild Rose?" Bennett asked.

"I'm guessing Kate knew Georgia was in trouble," Addie said. "My aunt has a special sort of sixth sense for people in need. I wouldn't be surprised if Kate let Georgia stay at Wild Rose when she was having problems with Lance. Kate probably even gave her a key. Lance would have known Kate and Georgia were friends. It wouldn't have been strange for him to find Georgia at Wild Rose late at night."

Addie's gaze met Georgia's.

"How close am I?" Addie asked. "Is it true?"

Georgia nodded. "I had no idea that my friendship with your aunt would end up hurting her. She was good to me. I'm so sorry." Her eyes filled with tears. "I'm so, so sorry."

"And what about Kate's notebook? Did you take it or was that Lance?"

"I didn't take it," Georgia said. "I found it, but not where I said. It was inside the store. I . . . I guess at that point I should have known Lance had done something awful."

Officer Davis placed his hand on Georgia's back and pointed to his car. "We're going to need to ask you some questions at the station."

She nodded and dropped her head.

Chelsea put her arm around Addie's shoulders. "Let's get you home, hon."

Addie was quiet on the way back to Stargaze. It was good to finally understand what had happened to Kate, but Addie still had to find proof. Georgia hadn't seen the attack, and Lance obviously hadn't confessed it to her, so she was really no help.

At least Lance was in custody.

Bennett drove to the bank, where Addie's car still sat on the curb outside the lot. He'd been summoned to the police station to give a statement about the night Lance had jumped him. The police already had the footage from outside Bennett's office. He expected they'd get a warrant to search Lance's home and RV, looking for the clothing he'd had on in the video and also the bat he'd brought to the alley when he'd come after Addie.

"Maybe Lance will confess to the attack on Kate," Addie said as she steered through downtown to Pine Avenue.

"He might," Chelsea said.

"He should. It would be the right thing to do. I don't think he's the kind of person to do the right thing, though. I mean, he was going to beat up his pregnant girlfriend. He fractured Bennett's ribs. He came after me with a bat."

Addie shivered at the memory of the dark figure looming over her in the alley.

Chelsea sighed heavily. "He's not a good person. He's not purely evil, but he's pretty messed up."

"You saw his aura?" Addie glanced at her friend.

"Yeah. It was . . . ugly. He wasn't always that way."

"He just oozes aggression, though," Addie said. "Even I can see that, in retrospect. The music he listens to is loud and angry. He drives that ridiculously jacked-up truck, like he's hoping for the chance to run over something small and defenseless. The few times I saw him in Ripped, he looked like he wanted to punch something. Maybe he's on steroids."

"It wouldn't surprise me. I heard rumors he was dealing drugs out of the store."

Addie shook her head. "My poor aunt just wanted to help Georgia."

Chelsea squeezed her shoulder sympathetically as Addie eased to a stop in front of Wild Rose Teas and Apothecary and turned off the engine.

"Hey, I bet you haven't eaten all day," Chelsea said. "Why don't you go inside, and I'll run down to Grinning Catfish and grab us some dinner."

Addie looked at her phone, suddenly realizing the sun had disappeared behind the building across the street. "Wow, it's after seven o'clock. I had no idea it was so late. Thank you for offering, that would be nice. I'll take Lucky out and then get him fed."

Chelsea headed off toward the brewery, and Addie let herself into the shop. Lucky bounced around in front of her, equally happy to see her and eager to get outside. She snapped the leash on and walked him down the street until he relieved himself on a fire hydrant.

"Oh, that's so cliché, little guy," she said with a little smile.

Back at Wild Rose, she went upstairs to pour him a bowl of kibble. Chelsea texted saying the food would take a while, as she'd put in their order right behind a large group, so Addie was surprised when there was a knock at the door a few minutes later.

When she went down, there were two silhouettes out front. One she recognized as Betty, with the customary high bun on her head and loose-fitting dress.

The other was a woman, but Addie wasn't sure who it was at first. She flipped on the shop's front lights and then stopped dead in her tracks, staring.

"Aunt Kate?" The words barely came out a whisper, as Addie seemed unable to pull a breath.

The woman lifted a hand and waved, smiling.

Addie ran to the front, yanked back the bolt, and threw the door open.

"Addie," Kate said, her eyes shining. "I'm so glad you're here."

"Oh, Aunt Kate, not as glad as I am," Addie said around the lump in her throat.

She squeezed her eyes closed against the tears that threatened and pulled her aunt into a long, tight hung.

When Addie finally let go and stood back, she realized Kate had changed. Her skin was pale, with a faint-green pallor. And her eyes were red-rimmed.

Addie reflexively retreated a step. "Are you . . . are you a . . ."

"Yes, dearie, she is," Betty said. She'd come into the store, too.

All Addie could do was stare and shake her head slowly for a few seconds, trying to process that Kate was there, alive.

Well, alive-*ish*.

Lucky was running rings around the three of them, so Addie made the introduction. He sat in front of Kate and let her scratch behind his ear.

"What happened?" Addie asked, spreading her hands.

Kate gave a little laugh, a cheery tinkling noise that Addie always loved. Her aunt had always been quick to smile and laugh.

"I regret to say that I'm not completely sure," Kate said. She touched the area above her temple. "I vaguely remember getting conked on the head. Then I woke up this morning in the home of a friend, and I was starving." She gripped her stomach.

Addie tried not to cringe. "Did they, uh, feed you?"

"Oh yes," Kate said with a quick grin. "Don't worry about that."

"From what Bennett told me, this transition was supposed to take longer," Addie said. "It's only been a few days. How did you do it so quickly?"

"I'm told I helped things along by dying."

Addie's fingers flew to her mouth.

"It's okay," Kate said gently. "I was lucky Hank was there."

Lucky let out a little yip at the sound of his name, and Kate bent to pet his head.

"Hank?" Addie asked.

"He's a Shuffler. A friend of mine. I'd wanted him to meet you, so he came here that night. Good thing he did, or I'd be . . ." Kate drew her finger across her neck.

Addie shook her head. "So, wait, this Hank was here the night you were attacked?"

"He wanted to keep a low profile, so I told him to go around to the alley. They—well, I guess *we*, now—are cautious like that," Kate said. "I came in the front and went to prop the alley door open. I told him to wait back there while I locked up, and we were quiet because I figured you were asleep upstairs. I intended to wake you up and bring you down to meet him. But then." She knocked her knuckles against her head.

"Why didn't Hank stop the attack?" Addie asked.

"He came in after it happened. He feels terrible about that," Kate said.

"So, when I ran out for help, he came in and took you away."

"That's how he tells it. I don't remember that part, of course." Kate shrugged.

"He turned you into a zombie," Addie said, not quite sure how she felt about this Hank person.

"He did. And it saved me," Kate said.

"Wow," Addie said. She faced Betty. "You knew where she was?"

"Not at first," Betty said. "But when you started talking about a secret community west of here, I had my suspicions."

"I'm sorry I got so mad at you," Addie said.

"No need to apologize, dearie. I'd have been incensed, too, in your position."

"Why did you leave that morning?" Addie asked Kate. "Bennett saw you go on foot toward west Stargaze."

"Ah, Bennett." Kate grinned again. "I'm glad the two of you met."

"But what were you doing so early in the morning?"

"There was an emergency shipment Shuffleville needed picked up," Kate said.

"But your car was here. You didn't have your purse."

"We were taking Carlotta's cooler truck, so we didn't need my car anyway," Kate said.

"Carlotta is head of Bowl of Plenty," Betty explained.

Kate rolled her eyes at herself. "I didn't know where I'd left my purse. I'm such a scatterbrain! All I had with me was a spare key to

Wild Rose. Anyway, we use Carlotta's refrigerated truck to get, well, you know . . . " She trailed off.

"It's okay, you can say it," Addie said. "Brains?"

Kate nodded. "Brains."

Addie moved to one of the café chairs and sat down heavily. "I was so worried when I couldn't get a hold of you."

"I'm sorry about that," Kate said. "I had no idea where I'd left my purse and didn't have your number memorized."

"Well, I found your purse." A giggle threatened to bubble up Addie's throat, and she couldn't hold it in.

"What's so funny?" Kate asked.

The giggles turned into laughter. Tears sprang to Addie's eyes. She doubled over.

"It's not funny," she finally choked out. "It's not funny at all. I really shouldn't be laughing."

Betty and Kate just stared at Addie, perplexed.

When Addie finally got a grip, she wiped under her eyes. "I may have accused Zelda of murdering you."

Kate's mouth fell open.

"And, um, I briefly thought Lisette might have done it, too," Addie said, and started giggling again.

"Good gravy, I've missed a lot," Kate said.

"You have no idea." Addie shook her head, her mood sobering. "But we did figure out who must have attacked you. I'm just hoping you can remember something to identify him."

Before she could launch into the story, Chelsea appeared at the door. She dropped the bag of food in surprise when she caught sight of Kate.

Addie hurried to let Chelsea in. After a quick explanation, some gasps from Chelsea, and more hugging, all four women went upstairs with the bag from the brewery.

The food sat forgotten on the little dining table while Betty and Kate settled on the sofa and Chelsea and Addie pulled over two chairs.

Addie told the story of her encounters with Georgia, Bennett getting beat up, almost getting attacked in the alley behind Wild Rose, and finally tracking down Lance and witnessing his arrest.

"And there's one more element of this," Addie said tentatively, her gaze trained on her aunt. "It's a little hard for me to talk about, but I think you need to know about it. I accidentally did a tea-leaf reading, and something very strange happened."

Smoothing her hair back, she took a deep breath, trying to settle the butterflies in her stomach.

Chapter Twenty-Three

ADDIE DID HER BEST TO talk about the tea-leaf readings without cringing. She described the sensations and symbols and how the tea leaves had ultimately led her to figure out Lance was responsible for all the violence in the neighborhood.

"I think the flower in the bottle must have been a symbol for you," Addie said to Kate. "That was the last one I couldn't figure out. But I think it's a symbol of your life having been preserved by your transformation."

Kate tilted her head. "I realized when you were a teenager that something was emerging within you. That summer, the one before your father put the kibosh on your visit, I saw it for sure. This ability comes from my side of the family, you know."

Addie nodded slowly. "I figured it did. When I handled your apothecary notebook, I got the same weird buzzing in my body."

"We come from a long line of witches, Addie."

Witches? That was a lot to try to process.

"Do you have some sort of ability that helps you create your remedies?" Addie asked, skipping over the part about her supposed witch lineage.

"Yes. I think of it as heightened intuition, but it's really more than that."

"I tried to tell her she had a gift," Betty said, her expression sad. "But she wasn't ready to hear it."

"I still don't know if I'm ready for that," Addie admitted, glancing at the mystic and then turning back to Kate. "All I really care about right now is that it helped me figure out who hurt you. And it reassured me you weren't dead. Even though I didn't understand that part at first, it *was* a small comfort, and I'm grateful for that. No offense to anyone in the room, but I'm not crazy about things I can't explain."

"I know," Kate said. "But I still have hope you might eventually want to embrace it."

"Well, for now, I think we should focus on anything you can remember," Addie said. "It'd really help if you could identify Lance, because I have a feeling he's not going to confess to attacking you. And what he did to you was the worst of all the attacks. That was a fatal hit to your head. I mean, it *would* have been fatal if not for your friend."

Addie had to stop talking. She pressed her fingers to her lips as tears pricked at the backs of her eyes.

"Addie's right," Chelsea said. "He'll be punished for the attacks on Bennett and Addie, but the most serious charge is the one that involves you."

Taking a breath, Addie composed herself. "Do you remember anything at all, Aunt Kate? A glimpse of his face? Clothing? Tattoos?"

Kate's gaze unfocused as she stared at a point on the ceiling for several seconds.

"I remember . . . shoes. I think," she said. "When I was lying on the floor, he walked past me. The cash register fell on the floor, and

I thought, oh man, if he broke that register, I'm really going to be mad."

"What do you remember about the shoes?" Addie prompted, gently trying to get Kate back on topic.

"Right. The shoes." Kate drummed her fingertips over her lips. "They were sneakers. Black with a white design on the side."

"Okay, that's good," Addie said. "Anything else?"

Kate lowered her eyelids. "E and W." Her eyes popped open.

"What does that mean?" Addie asked.

Her aunt shook her head. "I don't know. I just remember E and W."

Addie straightened, her eyes widening.

"I think I know what that might be." She picked up her phone and found an image of a compass showing the four cardinal directions that was similar to Lance's ankle tattoo. She covered North and South with her hands. "Like this?"

"Yes, something like that." Kate shrugged a shoulder.

Exchanging a glance with Chelsea, Addie licked her lips. Kate had seen a sliver of Lance's tattoo.

"Aunt Kate, I think that's enough to identify him," Addie said.

She dialed McCann. Even though it was after dark, the detective answered on the second ring and requested Kate come to the station.

Then Addie called Bennett.

"My aunt is back," she told him. "And she can identify Lance as her attacker."

"She's back?" he crowed.

Addie grinned. "Yeah. We're about to leave for the police station."

"That's amazing news. The best I could have wished for. Is she .. . ?" He trailed off.

"She's one of them," Addie confirmed. She let out a tiny, ironic laugh. "It saved her life. So to speak. Do you want to come over after we're done with the police?"

"Sure, I'd love that," Bennett said.

Betty decided to go home for the night, and Addie went to embrace her.

"Thank you for bringing her home," Addie whispered, taking in the mystic's familiar scent of rose water and incense.

"Of course, dearie," she said. "We'll talk soon."

"Say, do you happen to have any foundation I could put on my face?" Kate asked. "My pallor is going to look even more pronounced under fluorescent lights."

"I've got some tinted moisturizer," Addie said and went to get the tube out of the bathroom.

She tried not to stare as Kate used the product to mask her greenish skin.

"That smells nice," Kate said, looking down at the tube. "I'll have to pick up some for myself. Some of those eyedrops that get the red out, too."

Chelsea and Kate got into Addie's car, and she drove to the police station. Chelsea decided to stay in the car, so Addie went in with her aunt and found Detective McCann was waiting for them at the front desk.

She narrowed her eyes, peering at Kate. "Where have you been since the attack?"

"With friends," Kate said, leveling her gaze at the detective.

"Why didn't you report it right away?"

"I was traumatized."

What could Detective McCann say to that? Harassing the victim would be a very bad look for someone in her position. A little ping of satisfaction zipped through Addie when McCann dropped her line of questioning and led them through the station to the conference room in the back and didn't even try to challenge Addie's presence.

Kate described what she remembered, and McCann wrote in her little notebook.

"We're holding the accused here in the station's jail," the detective said. "Would you be willing to take a look at the tattoo to further verify it's the one you remember?"

"Absolutely," Kate said without hesitation.

"I'm going with her," Addie said. "For moral support."

She didn't think Kate truly needed the support. But Addie wanted to get one more look at Lance, with jail bars in between them, just to cement in her mind the knowledge that he was in police custody.

"Follow me," Detective McCann said, rising and going to the door.

She took them to the back of the building past where an officer was taking mugshots of a red-faced, haggard-looking woman around Addie's age.

The officer on duty at the jail's entrance buzzed them through, and McCann led the way past several empty cells.

"Not too busy today, huh?" Addie asked.

"We don't usually keep anyone here longer than overnight," McCann said. "Prisoners get transferred to the larger county jail."

They arrived at a cell where a man sat on a bench with his elbows on his knees and his head down. Addie recognized his red t-shirt from when she'd watched him get arrested.

"Hey." She pointed at his feet and turned to Kate. "Are those the shoes?"

Lance looked up, paling when he caught sight of the three women. His eyes popped wide when he saw Kate. He swallowed hard.

Kate leaned forward, squinting. "Yep. Those are exactly like the shoes my attacker wore."

"Tons of people have these shoes," Lance said. He was going for a dismissive tone, but his voice shook ever so slightly, spoiling his act.

"Come forward," McCann commanded.

For a second, Addie thought he was going to refuse. But then he slowly rose and trudged toward them.

"Pull up your pant legs," McCann said.

When he lifted the legs of his jeans, he revealed short socks.

And the compass tattoo.

"Turn a bit to your right," Kate said.

His jaw clenched, but he did it.

"That's the one," Kate said. "I saw that tattoo when I was on the floor, right before I passed out."

Not passed out. Died. But Addie sure as heck wasn't going to say that in front of the detective.

Not that Addie wouldn't like to see Lance punished for murder, but with Kate breathing and walking around and not obviously dead, the best they'd probably get would be something like attempted manslaughter, if her memory of crime TV shows served.

Anger tightened Addie's chest. She'd nearly lost one of the most important people in her life because of this man.

"You're a despicable person, you know that?" Addie said, her emotions bubbling over. "What kind of man goes after his pregnant girlfriend, intending to beat the crap out of her? Your rage and muscles and protein bars don't make you a man. They just make you pathetic."

His face tightened, and red splotches bloomed on his cheeks. He took a swift step at Addie, obviously meant to intimidate her, but she didn't budge.

"You are pathetic," she said quietly and slowly, staring him straight in the eye. "*Pathetic.*"

He grabbed the bars. "She cheated on me!" he growled.

"Yeah, I wonder why," Addie said. Shaking her head, she turned and walked away.

Lance ground out a string of curses at her, but she didn't care. He was behind bars. He was going to be punished. Maybe not to the extent he deserved, but she was satisfied that justice would be done.

———◦⁓⁓⁓◦———

WHEN THEY GOT BACK TO Wild Rose Teas and Apothecary, Bennett's Jeep was parked in front.

Kate went to embrace him.

"Thank you for all you did," she said. "I'm so sorry you got hurt."

"That wasn't your fault," he said, pulling back and looking down at Kate with genuine affection. "I'll heal. I'm just happy to see you back where you belong."

"I'm happy to be here," Kate said, but Addie thought she caught her aunt's smile slip a bit.

Once inside, Kate put some hot water on and made tea for everyone. Addie watched her aunt moving around the shop. She appeared lost in thought.

"She seems tired," Chelsea whispered.

"Yeah," Addie said, but she thought there was something more than just fatigue going on with her aunt.

Once the four of them were crowded around a small table, Addie took a deep breath. There were so many questions.

"Do you feel different?" she asked Kate.

Her aunt nodded. "Quite. It's hard to explain. Well, not all of it is hard to explain. My sense of smell is heightened. That's pretty straightforward. But there are other things."

"Are you . . . hungry?" Addie asked, her brow furrowing with worry.

She hated to think of Aunt Kate as dangerous, but the memory of getting caught up in the crowd behind the barriers made Addie's pulse bump.

"No, I'm okay for now," Kate said. She drew a slow breath. "But I'm a baby Shuffler. A newborn, really. I still have a lot to learn, and as one of them, I'm, well, I'm obligated to live with the others."

Addie sat back with a frown. "You can't live here? But what about the store? Your clients? This is your home."

"Well, there's still a lot to work out, but I'm hoping I won't have to give up Wild Rose entirely."

Addie just stared at her aunt in shock. Aunt Kate without Wild Rose or Wild Rose without Aunt Kate . . . it was impossible to imagine.

"You can live here, though," Addie insisted. "If you have to go back to west Stargaze, or Shuffleville or whatever, to get br—*food*, you can do that, right? You can't just give up your business. What would you do for money? What do the rest of the Shufflers do for money, anyway?"

"Well, many of them have jobs they can do from home, thanks to the internet," Kate said. "Some have businesses that can flex around the lifestyle. They all support each other to make sure everyone has what they need."

Addie couldn't bear the thought of Kate losing the shop.

"How about if I run Wild Rose until you can come back full time?" Addie offered.

"You'd do that?" Kate asked, hope lighting in her bloodshot eyes.

Addie hadn't really planned on staying in Stargaze long-term, but how could she leave now?

"Of course," Addie said.

"I'll help out however I can, too," Chelsea chimed in.

Addie squeezed her friend's hand in gratitude.

"You know I'm on board as well," Bennett said.

Kate beamed. "Thank you so much, that means the world to me."

Bennett nodded. "Well, you mean a lot to your clients and friends."

Again, Addie thought she saw her aunt's smile waver the tiniest bit. Maybe Kate was just overwhelmed by the outpouring of support.

"What else do you need, though?" Addie asked. "I mean in terms of, you know being a . . . Shuffler."

"I'm not really sure yet," Kate said. "This is all very new to me."

"I'm bummed you can't stay tonight," Addie admitted. "It's so wonderful to have you back."

Kate tilted her head, looking down into her mug. "I know. I wish I could just move right back in and go on with things as before. But we can chat for a bit before I have to go. Hank will be by to get me, in oh"—she leaned over to look at the time on Addie's phone—"half an hour or so."

Bennett pushed back from the table. "You know what? I think you and your niece should use that time to catch up."

Chelsea reached for her bag, which she'd dumped on the table behind her. "I was just thinking the same thing," she said with a kind smile.

"No, you guys don't have to go," Addie protested, but part of her did wish to have some time alone with her aunt.

"We'll have other opportunities to hang out," Chelsea said, giving Addie a quick hug. "Text me tomorrow."

Chelsea and Bennett left, and then Addie bolted the shop door. She came back to sit across from Kate.

"It seems like something is bothering you," Addie said quietly. "Do you want to talk about it?"

Kate pressed her lips together and swirled her tea a bit.

"Something has changed, Addie," she said. "And it's not just that I'm a Shuffler. Something I had before seems to be gone, and it's yet another reason I may need to give up Wild Rose Teas and Apothecary."

Chapter Twenty-Four

ADDIE'S BROW FURROWED IN CONCERN as she took in the seriousness of Aunt Kate's expression.

"Why do you think you'll have to give up the shop?" Addie asked.

"I think my magic is gone," Kate said.

Addie blinked, at first not sure what her aunt meant. "You mean the special thing you use when you make remedies for your clients?"

Kate nodded.

Addie's first instinct was to brush off the whole idea of magic. But she paused and then picked her words carefully.

"But don't you make effective remedies because of your expertise with herbs and natural remedies? That's not magic. That's experience and knowledge. And unless your, um, transformation took away what you knew, you still have that."

"Experience and knowledge play a part, but the special sauce is something else," Kate said, her voice growing passionate. "Something that seemed to come from my heart and soul, infusing the remedies and elevating them. Making them not just medicinal but truly healing on a level that's hard to explain."

"How do you know it's gone?" Addie asked.

Kate placed a hand on her chest. "I just feel it." Her lips trembled, and her eyes held true sadness.

Suddenly, Addie felt horribly guilty for wishing away the visions and whispers, for wanting to deny what she'd experienced with the tea leaves, when Kate seemed to be grief-stricken over the loss of a similar ability.

Addie reached out and grasped Kate's hand.

"Maybe with time it'll come back," Addie said gently. "Maybe once you've adjusted to this change, to your new life. Like you said, you're a baby zombie. When the shock of the transformation wears off, perhaps your magic will return."

She didn't even stumble over the word "magic," and Kate seemed to take a little comfort in the suggestion.

"I suppose it's possible," Kate said. "Only time will tell."

"Yes," Addie agreed. "Don't write it off until a little time has passed. Give yourself a chance to adjust."

"Thank you," Kate said, managing a smile.

"And in the meantime, I'll be here," Addie said firmly. "I'll do everything I can to keep the place running until you're ready to take over. No matter how long that takes."

Leaning back, Kate started to shake her head. "I can't ask you to do that. I know this isn't what you envisioned for the next stage of your life."

Addie let out a short laugh. "Maybe not, but the truth is, I wasn't totally sure where I was going next—literally or figuratively. And who knows how long it'll take me to figure it out? Besides, I'd rather be here for you. I remember a lot about your herbs and remedies from years past, but you can train me some more and I'll do my best for your customers."

But even as Addie said the words, her heart pinched a little. At first, she wasn't sure why. She genuinely wanted to help Kate and would never consider leaving her while she was in need. But in the few days Addie had been in Stargaze, something had started to take root in her mind, something she'd been too busy to truly focus on: her childhood dream of becoming a doctor.

In that moment, she realized she hadn't completely given up the dream. Some part of her had recognized that getting cut loose from her engagement, her job, and her life in San Francisco had allowed space for other possibilities.

But there was no way Addie could abandon her aunt. If the dream of going to medical school was a real one, it would still be there later.

Forcing a smile, Addie squeezed her aunt's hand.

There was a soft rap at the front, and Addie jumped, her gaze whipping up.

Kate twisted around to see who was there. "Oh, that's Hank." She hopped up, hurried to unlock the door, and then threw it open.

"Come in, come in," Kate invited. She trilled a laugh and clapped her hands. "You have to meet my niece."

Addie's brows lifted a bit as she took in Kate's beaming smile and the happy lilt in her voice.

The man who walked through the door was tall, broad-shouldered, and right around Kate's age. He had sparkling brown eyes and wavy, nearly black hair combed back from his face with only a few gray hairs at his temples. He was dressed in jeans and a flannel shirt left open over a navy tee. He was really quite handsome.

"Hank, this is Addie," Kate said.

Addie went to grasp his outstretched hand.

"Nice to finally meet you, Addie," Hank said with a warm grin.

"You too," Addie said. "And I have to thank you for what you did. For saving Kate." She shook her head. "I can't ever thank you enough."

Hank turned his smile toward Aunt Kate and then met Addie's gaze again.

"She was afraid of how you would take all this, but it seems she was worried for nothing," Hank said.

Addie pushed a strand of hair behind her ear. "Well, I'm still trying to wrap my head around it, to be honest. I'm just so relieved, so grateful, to have her back."

She embraced Kate, holding her close for a long moment. She smelled like the herbal shampoo in the blue bottle, the kind that was in the shower upstairs and that Betty had bought. The smell was a comfort, a reminder that Kate was indeed there and okay.

"Would you like to take your purse with you?" Addie asked when she stepped back.

"Oh, yes, that'd be a good idea, wouldn't it?" Kate rolled her eyes at her own absentmindedness.

"I'd like to be able to get a hold of you," Addie said. "I'll go get your bag and phone, and you can take the charger that's behind the register."

She gathered up the items and presented them to Kate.

"I'm so sorry I misplaced my phone," Kate said. "I know that caused you a lot of unneeded worry the day you came here."

"No need to apologize," Addie said. "You had other things on your mind."

Things like a shipment of brains to feed to zombies. Addie tried not to cringe, but *eww*.

Hank walked Kate out to the SUV parked in front of Addie's car. She stood at the window, waved when they looked back, and then watched them drive away.

When she turned, Lucky was sitting and watching her. She knelt down, and he came to her wagging his tail.

"Looks like it's just you and me, buddy," she said, scratching his ear and then dropping a kiss on top of his head.

After taking the used cups to the sink, washing them, and setting them on the drying rack, she walked upstairs, feeling forlorn and not quite sure why.

It was wonderful to have Kate back, of course. But maybe that was it. Kate might not be truly back.

Addie got ready to turn in and curled up under a quilt on the daybed with Lucky lying alongside her.

Her phone lit up and vibrated, and when she reached for it, there was a text from Bennett asking how she was doing.

She texted back: *Fine . . . mostly.*

What's wrong? came his reply.

Things are a little up in the air with the shop. Kate isn't sure she'll be able to return to her usual post here. That seemed to make her really sad, and it makes me sad, too.

Addie thought about mentioning the magic aspect that Kate felt had disappeared but wasn't sure how to work that in.

I'm sorry to hear that. She might just need time.

Yeah, I thought that too, Addie replied.

I'm here if you need anything.

Addie smiled. *Thank you, Bennett.*

Not long after, she fell asleep.

THE NEXT MORNING, ADDIE SAT up in bed and checked her phone. There was a message from Kate saying she planned to come to Wild Rose that afternoon. She asked Addie to open the store if she felt comfortable doing so.

Knowing her aunt would be there later gave Addie a lift, and she bounced out of bed to get ready for the day. The next couple of hours flew past as she showered, dressed, ate a bagel with jam, and went through the pre-opening procedure she knew by heart from years past.

The only snag was the lack of cash in the register. Addie walked down to the bank branch two blocks away with Kate's business ATM card in hand, which she'd left in a drawer. She of course had no hesitation telling Addie the PIN for the account so she could pull out some cash for the till.

On the way back, Addie stopped in La Petite Patisserie for coffee and recognized the man who was two ahead of her in line.

"Hi, Bennett," she called.

He turned, smiled, and let the lady in between them go ahead so he could stand next to Addie.

"I'm opening the store in a few minutes, and Kate's coming by this afternoon," Addie said.

"That's great." He nodded. "You seem in better spirits today. Or maybe I misinterpreted your text last night?"

"No, you didn't misinterpret it. I was having a bit of a moment. But I do feel better today. I'm trying to be optimistic."

It was their turn to order.

"Good morning, Lisette," Addie said in a very deliberate tone when they reached the counter.

The baker gave Addie a withering look. "What can I get you?"

Addie gave her latte order, and Bennett requested his usual black coffee with room for cream.

"I've got it," he said, passing Lisette his credit card before Addie could protest.

Lisette raised a brow and peered back and forth between Addie and Bennett in a way that brought a faint flush of heat to Addie's cheeks.

"Thank you, Bennett," she said, ignoring Lisette's looks.

He walked her back to the shop and then turned and retraced his steps to go to his office.

She watched him go, thinking about how much he'd done for her in such a short time. He was a good guy. Better than good. Kate seemed to like him a lot, too.

Motion across the street caught her eye. Betty was waving from the front of her emporium. Addie smiled and waved back.

Next door to the emporium, Ripped was dark. What would become of the space now that its owner was in jail? Maybe a new proprietor would take over and open up a different store. Something quieter, Addie hoped for Betty's sake.

Addie put the cash in the register, flipped over the sign in the door so "Open" faced outward, and looked down at Lucky.

"We're officially open," she said.

He wagged and gave her a doggy smile.

Ten minutes later, a woman came in to buy a bag of peppermint and ginger tea.

"This is my secret weapon against indigestion," she declared as Addie rang up the purchase.

Not long after, a large box arrived at the door. Having helped Kate with shipments many times, Addie knew just what to do. She unpacked the contents—sealed foil packets of bulk herbs and various sizes of empty amber dropper bottles—and laid them out on the counter behind the register so she could double check the items against the order sheet.

A few more customers came, and by the time Kate arrived, Addie's stomach was growling from having missed lunch. But she ignored the hunger pangs because she was so glad to see Kate back behind the counter.

It was almost like old times, except for the heavily tinted foundation Kate was wearing to cover up the green tinge of her skin, and the eye drops she used frequently to help with the redness.

Addie recounted the morning's sales, and Kate reviewed the neatly laid-out shipment with approval.

When Kate picked up her apothecary notebook, running her fingers over the tattered cover with affection, Addie watched quietly, remembering that Kate's skin, eyes, and diet weren't the only things that had changed. Her face took on a wistful expression as she carefully turned through some of the pages.

"I felt . . . *something* when I handled your notebook," Addie said.

Kate looked up. "You did?"

Addie nodded and ran a hand down her bare arm. "It was similar to the sensation I had with the tea leaves."

"That's the magic," Kate said with a small smile.

"But why did I feel it with your notebook?" Addie asked, her curiosity winning out over her skepticism. "I didn't create the remedies that are recorded in it. I'm not the one who imbued them with—with magic."

"I can't explain with a hundred-percent certainty why you felt something, but I have a guess," Kate said, obviously choosing her words with care. "My guess is that you might have the same gift for healing that I do, one that's expressed through plants and herbs and other natural elements."

Chewing her bottom lip, Addie considered what to say next. Her comfort zone beckoned her, telling her to change the subject. But curiosity and love for her aunt pushed her in a different direction.

"I think . . . I think I'd maybe like to possibly see if you're right," Addie said. "Just, you know, because it might be interesting."

Kate's smile was so bright Addie couldn't help reflecting it back.

But before they could explore the topic further, the door opened and Detective McCann walked in.

She peered hard at Kate as she approached the counter, staring in a way that made Addie a little uneasy.

The detective gave her a nod. "I was in the area, and I thought I'd stop by and let you know in person that Lance Mercer has been officially charged. One count of aggravated assault and battery, one count of attempted aggravated assault, and one count of attempted manslaughter. They're all felony charges."

Addie's stomach tightened at the sobering reality of the news. Renaldo must have decided not to report the black eye.

"And what about Georgia?" she asked.

"The girlfriend is considering whether to add to the charges," Detective McCann said. "But I can't comment further on her case."

With a heavy sigh that contained a mix of emotions, Addie nodded. "Thank you for letting us know."

"You're welcome. Someone from the county most likely will be in touch as the case progresses." After one last piercing examination of Kate's face, McCann turned and left.

"Wow," Kate said. "That was a splash of cold water, huh?"

Addie peered at her aunt. "You don't seem angry about what happened to you."

"I'm not happy about it, of course, but I've been thinking. If Lance really had attacked Georgia, he might have killed her. At best, he'd have hurt her badly. But because Hank was here, I'm, well . . ." Kate looked down at herself and held out her hands. "I'm relatively okay. So, in a way, it was almost better that it was me and not Georgia."

Addie shook her head in wonder. "Aunt Kate, you have the best heart of anyone I know."

Kate closed her eyes and shook her head. "Oh, pish posh. I was lucky."

"I think we'll have to agree to disagree on our definitions of 'lucky,'" Addie said with a laugh. She turned to the shelves of herbs, teas, and tinctures. "What do you say we get started on my training?"

"Oh, my goodness, I have so much to teach you," Kate said with delight. "This is going to be fun!"

Addie couldn't help smiling back. She hadn't yet decided what she would do in the long term, and she still hadn't made up her mind about abilities, gifts, and magic.

But she knew one thing for certain. At that moment, she was grateful to be in Stargaze with Aunt Kate.

In Addie's next magical mystery, *Peppermint and Potions*, she lands herself in some serious hot water. After buying an herbal remedy Addie made, the mayor's wife turns up dead. Addie is the prime suspect! It's going to take more than magic to keep her from a life sentence. Look for *Peppermint and*

Potions, the next book in the Tea Shop Witch Cozy Mystery Series by Thora Bluestone!